Praise for Stuart Kaminsky's
A Fine Red Rain

"Plenty of sweaty-palmed suspense of the best sort ...Moving and admirable."

The Washington Post Book World

"Shades of Raymond Chandler and Dashiell Hammett! If you think Stuart Kaminsky doesn't have a feeling for the *best* of both authors, you are in for a surprise."

San Diego Union

"The formality of speech, tension of plot and air of inevitability give this novel a romantic Russian feel."

Chicago Sun-Times

"Stuart Kaminsky's novels about Russian Inspector Porfiry Petrovich Rostnikov have been among his finest works, and his new Rostnikov book, *A Fine Red Rain*, is certainly no exception."

The Orlando Sentinel

DEATH
OF A
DISSIDENT

Stuart Kaminsky

IVY BOOKS • NEW YORK

Ivy Books
Published by Ballantine Books
Copyright © 1981 by Stuart Kaminsky

ISBN-0-8041-0404-2

Manufactured in the United States of America

First Ballantine Books Edition: March 1989

Acknowledgments

Many former Muscovites now living in the United States contributed to the background of this book. My greatest thanks, however, go to Boris Vinocur, whose years as a special correspondent for the Soviet Agency News, *Moscow Pravda,* and *Moscow Evening News* gave him access to information and background which proved to be essential in bringing Moscow to life for me.

"And what if I am wrong," he cried suddenly after a moment's thought. "What if man is not really a scoundrel, man in general, I mean, the whole race of mankind—then all the rest is prejudice, simply artificial terrors and there are no barriers and it's all as it should be."

—Raskolnikov in *Crime and Punishment*, by Fyodor Dostoevsky

DEATH
OF A
DISSIDENT

CHAPTER ONE

Moscow winters are really no worse nor much longer than the winters of Chicago or New York. If they seem so, it is because Muscovites like to think of their winters as particularly furious. It has become a matter of pride, an expression of unnecessary stoicism somewhat peculiar to the Russian psyche.

In truth, when the snow falls for three or four days and the temperature drops to thirteen degrees, the huge plows radiate down the wide streets from Red Square, clearing the way for the well-bundled pedestrians, who show no particular discomfort as they flow around the machines and past the *dvornik*—the teams of husbands and wives with brooms who sweep the smaller streets and sidewalks. Two hundred feet below the ground and the snow, millions of Muscovites travel in the warmth of the Metro to their jobs or to stores to wait in line for a dozen eggs or a pair of Czech shoes that look like those in American movies. At night, the same people and the more than half a million students in the city travel quietly home.

It is the silence of winter in Moscow that most strikes a foreigner. The crowds of the day and evening are enormous, but they hum rather than shout. If one passes the Aleksander Garden at the foot of the Kremlin, however, one might hear the laughing voices of children, who have been skating through the day.

In the evening with the coming of darkness, most of the almost eight million citizens of Moscow stay in their apartments, and the city appears almost deserted except for the bored youth, tourists, criminals and those with enough money to venture to one of the restaurants or movie theaters within walking distance.

It was on such a night that Aleksander Granovsky paced the living room of his sixth-floor apartment on Dmitry Ulyanov Street, not far from Moscow University. Aleksander Granovsky, once a teacher, was now an enemy of the state. As he paced the wooden floor of his living room, the ceiling of the apartment below shook. Part of the fault was in the construction of the twenty-year-old building; bribes and bribe-taking had resulted in corners being cut and floors having less insulation than had been specified. However, part of the fault also belonged to Granovsky, who refused to put even an old rug on the floor to cut down the noise of his nightly pacing. The old Chernovs on the fifth floor had once complained to the manager of the building's housing committee and they had been visited by the K.G.B., the Committee for State Security—a rather extreme reaction, they thought, to so simple a complaint. As Granovsky became more famous in the neighborhood and the world for his dissident ideas, the Chernovs learned to suffer his noise in silence rather than risk another visit from the K.G.B. man with the flat nose who made them feel guilty. Besides, their complaint had had no effect on Granovsky's pacing.

Misha Chernov, who cleaned the benches and walks in Pushkin Park, never considered a direct confrontation with Granovsky, a tall, dark crow of a man who never smiled.

On this particular winter night, the Chernovs' ceiling shook more than ever, but they consoled themselves with the knowledge that their upstairs neighbor would be going on trial in a few days, and with any luck they would finally have their peace.

The Granovsky apartment was exactly like that of the Chernovs and the fifty other tenants in the building: two rooms and a small kitchen. The Chernovs and the Granovskys, however, were unlike most of the other tenants. There were only two Chernovs and three Granovskys. Some of the other apartments held as many as six tenants.

Granovsky's pacing stopped abruptly as his wife, Sonya, and his daughter, Natasha, came out of the second room of their apartment and faced him. He looked at them clinically. They were of a kind, thin and pale and frightened. Granovsky was driven to near fury by their fear, but he had learned to pretend not to notice it. It pleased him that in seventeen years of marriage his wife had no idea how much her concerned cow eyes infuriated him.

"We thought we'd go to Kolya's apartment for a little while," Sonya said so softly that he barely heard her. "That is, if you don't want us to stay and . . ."

"Dress well," he said automatically. "Ask Kolya and Anna if they are going to try to come to the trial."

"He'll come," Sonya said. "Anna cannot. It would be hard for her at work."

Aleksander smiled, a dark, serious smile.

"Kolya will sit in the back and hide among the old women, the widows, and old maids who have nothing to do but watch the young lose their freedom," he said. He looked at Sonya for an argument about her brother's courage but as usual got none.

"We'll be back soon," Sonya said, avoiding his eyes and checking Natasha's red knit hat. Granovsky nodded, turning his back on the two women, who left, closing the door as quietly as they could.

"Justice," he thought to himself, composing his trial speech as he resumed pacing, "is guaranteed us, but justice is not what we get." He would wait to write it down. So far he didn't like it. He moved to the kitchen and put on a kettle of water for tea and then strode to the window, where he parted the curtain and looked down into the street. He did not try to hide as he glared down with a sardonic smile at the K.G.B. man shivering in the street six floors below. Granovsky could see the winter steam freeze in front of the man's mouth. Granovsky pushed the curtain over to be sure the man in the street would see him and then turned to find his cup.

The trial speech had to be very brief, for he did not know how much they would let him say. He had to memorize the words and give them to his friends before the trial to be sure they would be smuggled out to the rest of the world. *Pravda* might give the trial no more than a few lines on the back page if it covered the event at all.

Granovsky had no doubt that he would be found guilty of anti-Soviet activity, consisting primarily of smuggling articles on the Soviet penal system out to the West for publication. It was not the outcome of the trial Granovsky wished or expected to affect. He was concerned with a matter of principle. What was important to him was that his words be given to the Western press, that he become an international figure, a rallying point for action and protest. Considering America's ideas of human rights, there was even the possibility that the Americans might be willing to trade his freedom for one of the Soviet spies they had. It would depend entirely on his speech and how much publicity he could generate.

The wording of the speech had to be emotional and precise. He could buy himself time and a little attention and sympathy at the trial by provoking the judge to anger. He considered the possibility of smoking during the trial, a gesture Judge Drinyanov would regard as extreme disrespect. Granovsky would feign surprise and innocence of the affront. But that was a minor gesture he couldn't allow himself to fantasize about. What he had to do was complete the speech.

Drinking his tea, he began to go through his worn copy of *Basic Principles of Criminal Legislation of the Union of Soviet Socialist Republics and of the Union Republics*, with the vague hope of discovering something he might quote ironically. He knew the principles too well to expect an idea simply to leap out at him, but perhaps a word or phrase might bring inspiration.

He was dropping an extra sugar lump in his still

steaming tea when someone knocked at the door. Granovsky was annoyed. He hoped it was not Sonya and Natasha back early. He had no patience for visitors and he had no time to spar with the K.G.B.

"All right, all right," he shouted, stirring his tea. The knocking continued. He gulped the hot liquid quickly, scalding his tongue. If it were the K.G.B., he might well be in for a night of harassment, and it would be good to have something warm in the stomach. The knocking grew louder.

Holding the law book in his hand, Granovsky strode to the door, fixing his most defiant expression, which would suffice for the K.G.B. or complaining neighbors. When Granovsky opened the door and recognized the person before him, the glare turned to a sardonic smile.

"This is a busy night for me," Granovsky said without any attempt to hide his impatience. "What do you want?"

The answer came before Granovsky could really register it. Something flashed from behind the back of his darkly dressed visitor. The flashing thing looked brown and alien and heavy, and it struck Granovsky in the chest. As a youth, a soccer ball had once struck him in the chest during a game at Sokolniki Recreation Park, taking his breath as this did. Granovsky opened his mouth and looked down at what had struck him and was now protruding from his chest. He could see his own blood forming on it, and he wanted to cast it away.

Granovsky could not scream. Something sweet and wet filled his throat. Still clutching the book in his hand, Granovsky staggered backward, wondering what to do about the thing in his chest. He had a vision of the

Golem. If he were to remove the thing from his chest like the star of the Golem, he was sure he would cease to be alive. Yet the thing in his chest was making it difficult to breathe and he had so much to do—a speech to write, tea to drink. He looked toward his visitor for help but realized quite logically as he backed into the kitchen table that his visitor would surely not go through the trouble of killing him only to turn around and help. It would not be reasonable. *Nichego*, he thought, using the Russian word for resignation, a word that meant a sigh. Things were not going right. Trying to hold himself erect, Granovsky's hand touched the cup of hot tea and he pulled back, instinctively letting the book in his hand fly across the room. It hit the window he had looked out of earlier, broke it and sailed slowly into the cold darkness.

Khrapenko had not been looking up at Granovsky's window when it broke, but he heard the crisp tinkle of shattering glass and turned his head upward to see bits of light falling toward the street. In the midst of the shards of glass flew a white bird, its wings fluttering. Khrapenko was fascinated. A bird in Granovsky's apartment had apparently crashed through the window and was flying to the earth. Just before the object struck the snow, however, Khrapenko realized that it wasn't a bird, but a book. He looked up at the light in Granovsky's window before hurrying to the book, which had landed open in the snow. The book was covered with blood. Khrapenko ran for the entrance of the Granovsky building, wondering what madness Granovsky was engaged in.

Khrapenko was twenty-eight years old and had been

in the K.G.B. for four years. His father before him had been in the K.G.B. and had known Beria. The elder Khrapenko had a reputation for loyalty and little intellect and had never risen very high above the lowest rank. His son was credited with carrying on the family tradition. The assignment to follow and watch Granovsky had been neither welcome nor unwelcome. It had been puzzling, but as always, he had questioned nothing and had taken the assignment as a possible sign of growing responsibility. Khrapenko did wonder why Granovsky had been allowed to go on the streets in spite of his impending trial, and he had been told that surveillance might lead to further evidence, and that letting Granovsky out would be a sign to the world of the fairness of Soviet justice. Besides, his superior had told him Granovsky welcomed the trial and would certainly not think of running away.

Khrapenko had followed Granovsky through the day and taken up his position opposite the apartment building a few hours earlier. He knew Granovsky was aware of his presence, had actually mocked him from the window, but that did not matter. Until the window broke, Khrapenko's single conscious thought had been the passage of the forty-five minutes until he would be relieved for the night. Now Khrapenko was running through the small lobby of an apartment building and up six·flights of stairs to confront a dissident he had no desire to know.

Granovsky might simply have gone mad in fear over his trial. Khrapenko was not sure of how to deal with a bleeding madman. The K.G.B. man's only recourse would be to arrest him at gunpoint. If he had to shoot

Granovsky, he was sure his K.G.B. career would be at an end.

Coming down the stairs was a figure in black who Khrapenko pushed past without looking. He hurried up the concrete steps two at a time, using the railing more with each flight and listening to the echo of his own footfall.

The hall on the sixth floor was empty. Either the neighbors had heard nothing or were too afraid to come out. The door to apartment 612 stood open, and Khrapenko approached it, panting and reaching for his gun. A distinct and broad trail of blood pointed along the wooden floor to Granovsky's body. The eyes were open, the mouth was angry and red, as if he had spat blood in wild fury. Cold air blew in through the broken window, but Khrapenko did not notice. His eyes fixed on the thing sticking out of Granovsky's chest.

Khrapenko knew he had to act quickly, efficiently, that his career might well be on the line. He put his pistol away and reached down to touch the body, to confirm to himself that the man was dead, and his hand came away covered with blood. He was convinced. His next step was to call headquarters, though his impulse was to dial 02, the police. He was on one knee near the body, looking around the room for a phone, when he heard the steps behind him and drew his gun again. He came within the thickness of a fly's wing of shooting Sonya and Natasha Granovsky. The older woman looked first at the gun, then at the stranger and finally at the body of her husband. Then she began to scream, and the girl at her side, little more than a child the age of Khrapenko's own sister, began to cry hysterically.

Khrapenko rose from the floor and put out a bloody hand to calm the women, but they screamed even louder, a series of shrieks that sent ice through his brain. It was only then that he realized the two women probably thought he had killed Granovsky.

"I just found him like this," Khrapenko said, trying to keep composed, remembering his career, his father. "I'm a government officer. Please sit down and I'll call for help."

The two women turned their eyes from him, and the younger one stopped screaming. They were looking at the ugly, rusty sickle that someone had plunged deeply into the chest of Aleksander Granovsky.

In Moscow, the investigation of crime is a question of jurisdiction, and the investigation of important crimes is an important question of jurisdiction. Minor crimes, and no one is quite sure what a minor crime is, are handled at the inquiry stage by the M.V.D., the national police with headquarters in Moscow. Moscow itself is divided into twenty police districts, each responsible for crime within its area. However, if a case is considered important enough, a police inspector from central headquarters will be assigned. The *doznaniye* or inquiry is based on the frequently stated assumption that "every person who commits a crime is punished justly, and not a single innocent person subjected to criminal proceedings is convicted." This is repeated so frequently by judges, procurators, and police that almost everyone in Moscow is sure it cannot be true. This assumption of justice is also made for military and state crimes handled by K.G.B. investigators, who determine for themselves if the crime is indeed a state or military crime. Major nonmilitary crimes, however, are within the province of the procurator's investigator, who is responsible for a *predvaritel' noe sledstvie*, preliminary police investigation.

All police officers in the system work for the procurator's office. The Procurator General is appointed to his office for seven years, the longest term of any Soviet officer. Working under him or her are subordinate procurators, who are appointed for five years at a time. The job of the procurator's office is enormous: to sanction arrests, supervise investigations, appear at trials, handle execution of sentences, and supervise detention. The Procurator General's office is police, district attorney, warden and if necessary, executioner. The procurators of Moscow are very busy.

Which is why Procurator Anna Timofeyeva was still at her desk in the huge central police complex called Petrovka, on Petrovka Street. Petrovka consists of two ten-story L-shaped buildings which most Muscovites regard with a combination of awe and fear. Procurator Timofeyeva's office was a small, sparsely furnished room on the second floor of Building #1. Below her were the kennels where the German shepherds stalked and sometimes barked restlessly when they were not on patrol. At two in the morning, most of the dogs were out, but Procurator Timofeyeva did not notice the time nor the absence of the dogs she could hear during the daylight hours. She was a thick box of a woman, about fifty, officious and hard working. She knew that she looked formidable in her striped shirt and dark blue procurator's uniform, and she wished to look formidable. Therefore she wore the uniform most of the time, though it was not required. On her desk, as she drank cold tea, was a pile of reports from investigators on various crimes which were her responsibility. The top report, #30241, was on a case of hooliganism in which a group of drunks in a café had refused to leave at the 11:30 closing time. Procurator Timofeyeva knew from the report that one of the drunks was a Party member. She would try to shame him before the judge, point out what terrible behavior that was from a Communist when such great difficulties existed in establishing a new moral order.

Exactly how extensive those difficulties were in the case of crime was somewhat of a mystery even to Procurator Timofeyeva since statistics were never made public. However, judging from the pile of reports on her desk, the difficulties were extensive. There were cases of theft, drunkenness, black market sale of typewriters, refusals to pay alimony, murder. The pile never got smaller in spite of the eighteen hours a day the Procurator put in. This particular pile would in fact get much larger before it became smaller.

The Procurator General himself had called her no more than half an hour earlier. She had listened, asking questions only when it was expected. The conversation lasted no more than five minutes, after which she called the Petrovka motor pool and ordered a police car to go to the apartment of Inspector Rostnikov and bring him in immediately. She had watched the yellow *Volga* with the blue horizontal stripe pull silently into the wide street from her window as she wondered why the murder of Aleksander Granovsky was being turned over to the police and not the K.G.B.

Rostnikov had been sleeping in his apartment on Krasikov Street not more than two blocks from that of the Granovskys when the knock had come at his door. He had been dreaming of bench pressing four hundred pounds and had been grunting under the effort. His pained groans had awakened his wife, who was sure he was dreaming of some terrible sight witnessed during some investigation in his past.

"Porfiry," his wife said, shaking him gently. "Porfiry, there is a policeman at the door for you."

Rostnikov woke slowly to the voice telling him the police had come for him. That, he felt sure, was nonsense. He was a policeman, and it was he who knocked at doors in the night. Gradually, the four hundred pounds floated away and he forced himself awake.

"Time?" he said, sitting up at the side of the bed.

"After two," Sarah answered.

He was about to ask if Iosif were up and then remembered that his son, their son, rashly named for Stalin in a moment of youthful patriotism, was in the army now and stationed somewhere near Kiev. Rostnikov pulled himself from the bed, touched his wife's cheek reassuringly and limped across the room. He was a powerful, compact man of fifty-two, who lifted weights to compensate his body for the injury to his leg. In 1941 he had caught a piece of metal in that leg during the battle of Rostov. It was so long ago that he didn't even remember what it was like to walk without dragging the leg behind him.

The young policeman was standing in the doorway, afraid to step into an inspector's home and track snow. He held his fur cap in his hand.

"You are to come with me to Procurator Timofeyeva's office immediately,'' the boy said almost apologetically.

Rostnikov rubbed his hand across his stubble and held the other up to indicate to the young man that he would be with him in a few minutes. The young policeman looked relieved.

After nearly thirty years as an inspector of police, Rostnikov knew better than to ask the young officer what it was about. The boy would have been told nothing. In five minutes, Rostnikov was out of his apartment, which was no larger than that of the dead Granovsky, and on his way to Petrovka. He tried to get back to his wonderful dream as he rocked in the back seat of the Volga, but the dream was gone. Rostnikov sighed, accepted its loss, and opened his eyes.

When he arrived at Procurator Timofeyeva's office, Rostnikov entered slowly after knocking and sat in the soft black chair across from the Procurator. She in turn sat behind her desk in a straight wooden chair. Rostnikov wasn't sure if she gave her guests the more comfortable chair to make them feel guilty about having greater immediate comfort or because she really preferred discomfort. He had come to the tentative conclusion that it was discomfort for herself she sought. Above her head, on the wall, was a picture of Lenin as a young man, emerging from his cell-like room with a wan smile. Rostnikov had long ago concluded that the picture was not just a political necessity but a source of inspiration to Comrade Timofeyeva. He sometimes imagined her as a happy convert to the religion of Communism. He had, however, learned to have great respect for her zeal and ability.

Timofeyeva looked across her desk at the investigator known widely as "the washtub." She offered him a cup of cold tea, and he accepted it, reaching out a rather hairy hand to take it in.

"What do you know of Aleksander Granovsky?" she asked, trying to ignore the pile of work on her desk and concentrate on this new problem. She did not think in terms of complaint. She was a loyal party member. If a task was given to her, it was necessary, and she would simply have to find the time for it. Her doctor had warned her about her work load and her heart, but she had decided to put aside the occasional pains she felt, which he had told her were warnings to slow down and relax.

"I've read the papers, heard the news," shrugged Rostnikov, still wearing his coat pulled snugly around him. Comrade Procurator's office was always cold.

"Granovsky is dead," she said. "Murdered. At about eleven, someone went to his apartment and plunged a rusty sickle into his chest. Apparently, it was a madman who also threw a law book through the window before he fled."

"His trial was to have been the day after tomorrow?" Rostnikov asked.

"Yes."

"Can I ask why he was not in prison?"

"He welcomed the trial," Timofeyeva said, drinking some sugarless cold tea. "It was decided to be a good gesture."

"The K.G.B.?" Rostnikov tried.

"They were watching him," she said slowly, "but they did not see who killed him."

"And the K.G.B. doesn't want to handle the investigation?" Rostnikov went on, knowing he was treading dangerously.

"What do you wish to discover, Tovarisheh?" she said with a cold look, which did nothing to intimidate Rostnikov, who was suddenly very hungry.

He sighed and plunged in:

"It seems coincidental to me that he should be allowed out of prison before his trial, that he should be killed so close to that trial and that the K.G.B. should not want to handle the investigation."

"You think the K.G.B. might have killed him?" she said.

"No," said Rostnikov. His stomach growled loudly. "If the K.G.B. wanted to get rid of him, they would be more careful, considering who he was, but a single agent provoked by a man like Granovsky might . . ."

"I see your point," said the Procurator, folding her hands in front of her. "You will and do have permission to delicately make inquiries in that direction, but very delicately, you understand?"

"Very delicately," he agreed. "A sickle, you say?"

"Yes, a sickle."

"Symbol of the revolution," he said softly.

"There is no accounting for the variances of the Muscovite mind," she said without humor. "I have seen too much to try. Take it where you will, but remember the problems. You have the direct order of the Procurator General himself on this investigation. The world will know of this murder in a few hours. There are many in other countries and in our own who

16

will be convinced that some force in the government is responsible.''

"And,'' said Rostnikov placidly, "if they turn out to be correct?''

"Then,'' she said, turning to her picture of Lenin for inspiration, "we will discuss it again. But assuming it is not, when we catch the murderer, we must have unshakable evidence of his guilt which the Procurator General can release and use to remove any conspiracy accusations. You understand?''

"Fully,'' said Rostnikov, pushing himself up from the soft chair with effort. "I can expect the K.G.B. people to be hostile to my investigation. I can expect the friends of this Granovsky to be hostile because they distrust us and fear for their own safety. I can expect neutral witnesses to hide and pretend they know nothing. In short, a typical murder.''

"Yes,'' she said, turning back to face him. "Except we do not have a great deal of time. The faster we know what happened, the sooner we can prevent any international incident over this. If we get nowhere in two or three days, we can expect the case to be taken out of our hands.''

"Which will not look good on our record,'' said Rostnikov without concern. Timofeyeva and Rostnikov exchanged very slight smiles. He had no hope of becoming a procurator and no desire to become one. He was too old, had a Jewish wife, and was quite content to be an investigator. If anything would prod him into extra effort, it would be pride.

"I have no doubt that you will do your best,'' she said.

"I will do better if you allow me to take Karpo and Tkach off the cases they are working on and assign them to this," he said, standing at the door.

The Procurator looked at the pile of reports on her desk. Five of them belonged to the two junior investigators in question.

"Take them," she said.

"Thank you," replied Rostnikov respectfully and left the cold office to search for something to drink before he called the two men who would be helping him find what appeared to be a very mad or very clever murderer.

CHAPTER TWO

At three o'clock in the morning, New York City is vibrating with neon, pulsating with bodies in doorways, and even the most remote streets of Queens are not surprised by a scream or laughter. At three in the morning, Paris streets are alive with casual strollers, policemen, and drunks. But at three in the morning, Moscow is a city of echoes and shadows, its streets deserted and silent. In Moscow the liquor stores close early, the restaurants at midnight, and the metros at one. A few taxis prowl the streets with three or four bottles of vodka under the front seat to sell at double the store price to thirsty insomniacs. Moscow begins work at five in the morning. The few hours before are for the criminals, the police, taxi drivers, government officials at parties, and party officials working on government.

At three o'clock this morning Viktor Shishko sat at his German-made typewriter in the office of Moscow

Pravda carefully wording a story on the death of Aleksander Granovsky. The only information he had was that given to him by Comrade Ivanov who, in turn, got the information from the Communist Party member who served as liaison with the various Russian investigatory agencies. Viktor wrote what he was told. It took him fifteen minutes. The next step was to drink some strong black coffee, look out the window at the snow, and wait, knowing that the story would probably be killed or rewritten by someone else even though it was and would be no more than ten lines at most. Even then the governing committee of *Pravda* might kill it entirely at their morning meeting. He considered going to the toilet, but sighed and decided to wait in the hope that the call might come through and still give him the chance to get a few hours of sleep. His neck felt gritty in spite of the cold draft from the window. He made a promise to himself to take a cold bath if the call came through and he got home within an hour.

At three o'clock that morning three very young men in black leather jackets and jeans were clearing out the back of a small truck. All three wore their hair long and brushed back like American pictures they had seen of James Dean or Polish pictures of Zbigniew Cybulski. Both Dean and Cybulski had died violently and young. At least two of the three young Muscovites half-longed for the same fate and imagined an underground reputation that they would not be around to experience. All three had taken American nicknames, "Jimmy," "Coop," and "Bobby," all three had guns, all three wore fixed smiles, all three were frightened by what they had been doing and were about to do.

At three o'clock that morning, Rudolt Kroft was cleaning his police uniform, which was odd. It was odd not because it was three o'clock in the morning, but because Rudolt Kroft was not a policeman. He lived in a four-story wooden building that sagged dangerously to the left, which may have been politically valid as a metaphor, but held no meaning other than structural for Kroft and the other tenants. Kroft, in contrast to his building, sagged to the right as a result of a circus accident many years before. He was still agile and a capable actor as evidenced by his successful role as policeman for the last few months, but he was also cold, very cold in his sagging building of outcasts and foreigners. It pleased him to stay warm by cleaning the uniform and thinking of his role for the coming day.

At three o'clock that morning Ivan Sharikov dropped his fare on Lenin Avenue and accepted the eighty kopeks fare, knowing he would get no tip. Party officials gave no tips and Ivan expected none. The fare, heavily bundled and in bad humor, had slipped getting out of the cab as he walked to his apartment door. Ivan, whose neck was fat and slow, turned away hiding a satisfied grin, and flipped on the green light in his windshield to show he was free to take another fare. He slowly put his taxi into gear and backed into the street slipping as the thin, nearly bald tires tried to grab the street and clawed only at ice.

Ivan's prospect of making any real money that night was slim, but he owed too much and knew he could not sleep anyway with the pain in his back. When the pain got really bad, he considered going to the clinic, but the clinic wait might be hours, and the doctor, if he even got to see one, would send him back to work with meaningless pills or worse, he would be sent to the hospital ward and lose his chance to make up some of the money he owed his brother-in-law. In the old days, even a dozen years ago, he could have told his brother-in-law what to do with his loan, but time had reversed their positions. Ivan had grown fat, old, and tired and Misha had grown lean, hard, and resentful from his years at the packing house.

Ivan's plan was to go back to the center of town in the hope of picking up another late-working middle-level government official. The really big officials would have their own cars. The little officials could not afford a taxi. The middle officials who lived on the fringes of Tolstoy Street could pay the price but were never good for conversation or a tip. As his tires caught ice and turned slowly, easing the taxi into the street, Ivan spotted a lone dark figure standing at the curb fifty feet away. The figure seemed to be waiting and swayed a little, perhaps drunk. Ivan's dull eyes squinted with the possibility of an easy fare and he drove forward toward the figure.

At three o'clock Porfiry Rostnikov made two phone calls and said ten words to each of the men he called:

"Rostnikov here, come to three-forty-four Dmitri Ulyanov Street. Apartment six-hundred-twelve."

Although he had been fully asleep when the phone rang, Emil Karpo had answered before the first short ring had finished bouncing off the walls of his small room. He said nothing when he heard Rostnikov's brief message followed by a click ending the connection.

Karpo looked at his clock in the dim street light from his undraped and unshaded window. It was three exactly and he would remember it if a report were called for later. Karpo remembered everything, every detail. This recall had started more than twenty years earlier to protect himself and it soon became so much a part of him that it was no longer conscious. His mind was filled with data, and his one bookcase was lined with notebooks full of observations which would probably never be called for or used. He stood up from his mattress, his dark body catching the dim light from the window. He dressed quickly, without looking. All his clothes were the same. He had two suits, both grey-black, both neatly pressed, both quite old. He had five shirts, all a dull white, all starched. He had three ties, all dark and unstylishly thin even for a Moscow which perversely prided itself on being five years behind the rest of the world in fashion, and he had the uniform of the male Muscovite, a long black coat and black fur hat.

Karpo knew who lived at 344 Dmitri Ulyanov Street, but he did no more than register the fact and feel the reinforcement of something like pride at having the information. He refused to conjecture or guess about what it might mean. Guessing was a waste of time and if anyone were to ask him what he thought was happening, he could honestly say he had no idea, at least no idea anywhere near the conscious level. Karpo was a man who kept his thoughts and his body to himself. He lived for his duty, coolly, and without humor. When he had started with the old M.V.B., he had quickly earned the nickname of ''The Tatar'' because of his slightly slanted eyes, high cheekbones, tight skin, and expressionless dark face. That was twenty years ago. Now, the younger men had taken to calling him "The Vampire" for many of the same reasons and his preference for working nights. He was, at six-foot-three, tall for a Tatar and not pale enough to be a vampire. Karpo had not a single friend, which suited him. He would tolerate no slackness in others and radiated cold, silent fury toward those who did not devote themselves fully to their tasks, particularly the seemingly endless task of cleansing Moscow. He also had many enemies among the continued offenders of what passed for an underworld in Moscow. And that too suited him.

Karpo had only one conscious secret, the savage headaches that came for no apparent reason and stayed for periods of an hour to half a day. The pills he had been given years earlier helped to control the pain to the point where he could work in spite of it. There were times he even welcomed the pain as a test of his body and mind, a test to prepare him for a greater pain from some unnamed enemy of the state at some unspecified moment in the future that would probably never come.

When he was fully dressed and had brushed back his dark thinning hair, Karpo stepped out into the hall outside of his small cell-like room. He closed the door quietly, setting the hair-thin wire that would later tell him if anyone had visited him or might be inside waiting when he returned. He expected no such visit and had never had one.

"Rostnikov here, come to three-forty-four Dimitri Ulyanov Street. Apartment six-hundred-twelve."

"What . . ." Sasha Tkach started to answer, but cut

himself off and began to say, "I'll be right there," but the line went dead before his last word.

The phone had rung six times in the two-room apartment. Sasha's mother slept no more than a foot from the phone in the bedroom but she was nearly deaf. He had really wanted the phone in the other room, the living room/kitchen where he and his wife Maya slept, but the phone had been installed when he was at work and he did not want to complain. The phone had been a sign of his priority, his standing as an investigator, a person to be respected, but it was a privilege one did not want to abuse. So the phone remained in the bedroom. He gathered his clothes quietly and went back out to the living room.

"You're going?" Maya said, sitting up on her elbows. She turned on the light. Her hair was long and straight and covered part of her sleepy face. She had an accent of the Ukraine. To Tkach, who was twenty-eight and had been married for four months, it still sounded exotic. She had come to Moscow to work as an accountant in the State License Bureau and he had met her there while doing a few days of investigation on a black market case. The case had been a success. They recovered four cartons of American blue jeans which had been turned over to the case procurator after Tkach committed the first legal violation of his adult life. He had taken one pair and given it to Maya.

"That was Rostnikov," he said, running his hand through his blond hair and pulling on his pants.

She looked at the clock. It was three and she would have to get up in an hour.

"Take your lunch in your pocket," she said. His

salary was two-hundred-fifty rubles, hers ninety rubles. They spent almost 70 percent of that on food and couldn't afford to have either of them eat any meals at restaurants.

He nodded, moved to her, kissed her lightly and touched his hand to her shoulder, indicating that she should go back to sleep.

If there was no delay on the Metro, he could get to Dimitri Ulyanov Street in twenty minutes. A cold cloud of snow came dancing down the street as he stepped out, wondering what might cause Rostnikov to call him so early. There was a night shift for emergencies. It must be something big.

At three o'clock a dark figure stood swaying on Lenin Avenue. He was not drunk. He was trying desperately to think, but all that would come to him was that he would go home and wait for her.

He knew he had been walking for—how long? Perhaps ten minutes, perhaps an hour or more. And there were many things to do, to plan, but they would not form into words and pictures. It had been like this when he was a child, but he was no longer a child. It was like trying to put ideas together when sleep is coming.

Logic was the proper recourse, think it through, come to a conclusion only after you had asked the right questions. That was what Granovsky had taught him. Maybe if he could phrase the question clearly, he could trick it, get it done and answered, and go on to other problems, go home and wait for her.

Through the snow flakes on his eyelashes, he looked up at the tall apartment buildings and felt dizzy.

The taxi was in front of him and a thick-necked man leaned out and said something. The voices that plagued him vanished and he looked at the man in the taxi.

"You want a taxi?"

He had never been in a taxi alone. In the past two years he had really only been in a taxi three times, always when someone else paid. Two of those times it was Granovsky who had paid. He climbed into the back of the cab, touching the seat, smelling the sweat of the day and trying to fix the blue-black face of the driver in the present.

"You drunk?" asked the driver with a sigh.

"No," he said, "I . . . I've been thinking and my mind is just . . . Take me to Petro Street."

"Where on Petro?"

"One three six."

"You want a bottle?" Ivan held up a vodka bottle pulled from under the seat. "Two rubles."

The passenger reached forward and took the bottle. He opened it in darkness as the cab moved slowly forward, and he drank deeply, waiting for the sting of cheap vodka. Maybe it would give him a moment, just a moment of clarity. He felt if he could just break through, be sure, there would be a tremendous surge of power, strength. He wanted to be fully awake and aware. A man cannot cope if he is not awake and aware, not in control. He had learned that from Granovsky. He did not want to be a dreamer. He had almost been lost in dream those years earlier at the hospital. But there had been no comfort in the dream. It had sucked him deeper and deeper, drowning, as he called for wakefulness and had not been heard. It had taken long, and his family had abandoned him at his father's decree. Slowly he had awakened and felt the touch of objects and people. He had gradually gotten better. Then he had met her, had met Granovsky. Granovsky had helped him. They had both helped him move from dream to reality, but he felt the tug of the dream again and knew he might slip back if he did not make a mighty effort. It had to be stopped. If he could be sure that he had done it, then it might stop. He drank from the bottle and this seemed to help.

"It's not the best, not American or Czech," said the driver, unable to turn his fat neck, "but it's not bad, right?"

The passenger said nothing. He thought. He would wait for her. But what if his father's voice were right? What if he hadn't done it? He leaned forward toward the sweat smell and solidness of the driver, who sensed him and was startled.

"My problem," said the passenger, "is that I'm not sure if I did something tonight. If I didn't do it, I can't take the next step. Each thing must come in order. To do one without having done the other would make me a fool. Do you understand?"

The driver grunted. He had hauled drunks and lunatics through the streets of Moscow for over thirty years and he had learned not to argue, simply to listen and agree. Ivan Sharikov had his own problem, the pain in his back that was too severe to ignore.

"Moscow is a city of pain," said the passenger.

"True," said the driver. The cab skidded on a patch of ice on the bridge across the Moscow River and spun slightly. The passenger said something else, but the driver was too busy with the skid to pay attention, though he caught the last few words:

". . . it again, but I couldn't go back, could I?"

"No," the driver agreed, "you couldn't."

For blocks the passenger was silent, and then fear came. He felt himself sinking into the dream. He felt panic and knew he had to talk, to claw with the fingers of his mind to stay in the world of cold and pain. In the rear-view mirror, Ivan could see the passenger sweating as if it were half time in a summer soccer game.

"You can't know what it is like. Something has to be done. I have to feel, touch, know I'm here. If I did it, I have a purpose, things to do. I can wait for her."

At best, drunk, at worst, mad, Ivan was thinking, and he sped up slightly, afraid of skidding but eager to get rid of the sweating, babbling passenger and get to his room where he could wrap a blanket around his back.

"If I act in this world, I stay in this world. You understand?"

"Yeah," grumbled Ivan.

"He told me that. Granovsky told me that, and he was right. I used to think the whole world was a fake, cardboard sets like a play with everyone acting their roles. I used to think there was another world quite different from ours, and I could get to it if I could just get past one actor on the street, just make it around a corner before they had time to set up another façade. I have a sense of that coming back now. There's no point asking you because if you're part of it, you'll lie. You see. I'm thinking logically again."

The passenger now leaned back into darkness and covered his face with his hands.

"It's logical," said the passenger. "The only way to know is to do it again and do it right and feel it, have evidence, blood, something."

"Right," said the driver, pushing the *Volga* to its swaying limit. "Just relax. We'll be there in a minute."

"Then rooms would not grow and things would feel," came the muffled voice from the rear followed by the sound of breaking glass.

"Hey," shouted the driver in anger mixed with fear, trying to look over his lump of a shoulder. "I just had that seat cleaned and . . ."

At the corner of Petro Street and Gorky Place, eighty-year-old Vladimir Roshkov and his fifty-year-old son Pyotr were about to cross the street on their way to their small clothing store. The basement had flooded and they wanted an early start to clean it up before the business day began. The taxi came around the corner sideways in a mad skid catching Pyotr's pants on a bumper, stripping him, and throwing him against a street light. Vladimir jumped back, looked at his startled son, and watched the taxi bounce over the curb and come to a solid stop against the wall across the street. Pyotr stepped forward dazed, bruised, and confused, and thought only of getting back home and putting on a pair of pants. Anger took a few moments to hit the father and son, who were strong, solid, and very slow of thought. When it came, it came to them both at the same moment and they strode toward the now silent cab. They took a few more steps forward and stopped.

The black figure was covered with blood, but it was not the blood that stopped them. It was the fact that the man was laughing softly, not the laugh of hysteria, but the laugh of gentle pleasure. The man looked at the two figures in front of him, one in the snow without pants, laughed and ran down Petro Street. By the time the Roshkovs recovered their wits and hurried after him, the man was almost out of sight. They stopped, panting, with no heart for the pursuit and headed for the taxi.

The wind was whipping Pyotr's bare legs, and his father could not help thinking this would mean the police and questions and hours lost in draining the basement. He opened the front door of the cab saying to his son, "Go call the police—"

As the door came open, the body of Ivan came tumbling out into the street, a lump of human with a face as red as his country's flag.

"Go, fast," said Vladimir, waving at his son and considering whether the two of them should simply run away. He decided that someone might have seen them by now and to run might make them suspects in this murder. As Pyotr hurried bare-legged across the street and back to find a phone, a groan or sound came from the heap of blood in the snow.

Vladimir forced himself to the side of the man and leaned forward.

"Yes," he said. "My son is getting the police. Don't worry."

"Granovsky," said Ivan Sharikov the cabman.

"Granovsky?" repeated Vladimir Roshkov.

Ivan nodded his bloody face in agreement and went silent.

"Are you dead?" said Vladimir Roshkov.

"I don't know," replied Ivan the cabman who promptly died.

The young police officer parked the yellow Volga in Dmitri Ulyanov Street and sat looking straight ahead the way he had been taught to do. He wondered why the Inspector did not get out of the car immediately and rush into the building, but he did not let his curiosity show with even the twitch of his face. He tried to think of nothing and was surprised at how easy it was to do so.

Rostnikov knew that once he plunged into this case—with pressure from above and a good chance that he would come up with nothing—the days and the nights would begin to blend, he would grow weary and irritable; he would be uneasy until he had a desk full of possibilities and a suspect to talk to. If it was to be as it had been in the past, these were his last moments of ease before embracing the agony of the investigation and the torment of other people's tragedies. He planned nothing. The case would define itself, carry him into branching streams and dead ends. He would float or fight as he saw fit, trying not to drown in paperwork and bureaucracy.

He thought of his son's face. It was a trick he used to relax. He forced himself to recall the boy's features, to let the nose define the face and the mouth, to remember him as a child of fourteen, lean and uncertain, and as a young man of twenty-four, solid and curious. The mouth always came to Rostnikov as a stern line that had to be modified by a great effort of will. With concentration, the face of his son came to him and he smiled, let it go and stepped out of the car. The pre-dawn air was sharp and cold and clean compared to the enervating warmth of the Volga.

"Turn off the engine," he said to the driver. "If you get cold, come inside."

Rostnikov moved into the building and up the stairs slowly. His leg would allow no other progress, but that did not disturb him. He knew that Alexiev, the strongest man in the world, could move no faster than himself. If Alexiev walked up four flights of stairs, his massive legs were in pain from chafing against each other. Strength was not a matter of swiftness but heredity, determination, and dignity. Dignity had a price. Rostnikov's hand touched an old peeling poster on the red brick stairway wall. "Surpass America . . ." it began and never ended. The area of competition was lost in the act of some young vandal of the past.

The officer in front of Apartment 612 was short, stocky, and dark. His collar was clearly rubbing his neck painfully. His winter cap was pulled down against his ears, which bent comically. The officer recognized Rostnikov and stepped out of the way.

"It's warm out here," said Rostnikov. "Open your jacket and relax. Who's in there?"

"Wife, daughter, Officer Drubkova," said the officer, unbuttoning his coat.

"The corpse?"

"Covered with a sheet. No one has touched it."

Rostnikov knocked and waited for a woman's voice that told him to come in.

An awkward move of the foot was all that kept him

from slipping in the sticky trail of blood, and even so, he almost fell. Only one of the three women in the room had looked up to see him enter. She was clearly Officer Drubkova. Her face was pink and eager. Her zeal would be oppressive and tiring. He knew her type as soon as their eyes met. She had been kneeling next to the corpse which was covered with a white sheet, a sheet that showed remarkably little blood, considering the broad trail of it in the room. The corpse must have been covered very recently, Rostnikov decided, fascinated by the clear outline of the sickle under the sheet.

A woman and young girl, with hands identically folded on their laps, sat in an uncomfortable-looking straight-back sofa of uncertain period looking at the white figure on the floor.

Officer Drubkova bounded toward him like an athletic bear and introduced herself, almost saluting.

"Officer Drubkova," she said. "The hospital has been alerted and will come for the body when you are finished. There is a hole in the window which I have covered with cardboard. We have touched almost nothing and I have retrieved a book that was thrown through the window."

She handed it to Rostnikov, who tucked it awkwardly under his arm not wanting it at all, but not wanting to offend her. Nor did he bother to tell her that it was pointless to avoid touching the room. If there were fingerprints, they would be on the handle of the sickle and nowhere else that would be meaningful. Any room is a maddening, useless fury of fingerprints.

"Very good," said Rostnikov. Officer Drubkova's pink face turned a pleased red. "Now go to another apartment and call the hospital. I want the corpse taken care of as soon as the photographs are taken. When you make the call, remain in the hall and do not let anyone in except Inspectors Karpo and Tkach. Do you know them?''

She nodded affirmatively.

''Good. I can count on you.''

Officer Drubkova hurried out of the room and Rostnikov opened his coat in relief. He glanced at the law book under his arm and placed it gently on the wooden table. He lifted one of the three wooden chairs at the table and moved it directly in the line of vision between the two thin women on the sofa and the body on the floor. The mother tried to look through him, found him too solid and then allowed something like anger to touch her face. That was what he wanted, some awakening and emotion, something to touch beyond grief. The young girl, however, simply stared through him.

''I'm Inspector Rostnikov. Porfiry Petrovich Rostnikov. My father enjoyed *Crime and Punishment* and named me after the detective. I've always thought it had something to do with my becoming a policeman.''

The woman allowed more anger to show.

''I am Sonya Granovsky and this is my daughter Natasha.'' Defensiveness and hostility were there, waiting for him to say the wrong thing, for she badly needed someone to attack, to blame.

''I have a son,'' said Rostnikov, looking at the young girl.

Sonya Granovsky's brown eyes looked at him curiously. This was not the conversation she expected.

"He's in the army now, but I don't think he likes it. Why would anyone in his right mind except Officer Drubkova like the army?'' he said in a whisper.

They fell silent as Rostnikov continued to look at Natasha.

"How old are you?'' he said softly.

The mother looked down at her daughter as if she had forgotten the girl was there and was curious about what the answer might be.

"I'd guess you are sixteen,'' Rostnikov said.

"Fourteen,'' the girl said, without refocusing her eyes.

Rostnikov sighed and spoke even more softly, so softly that it almost seemed that he was speaking to himself.

"My father died when I was fourteen,'' he said. "For a few years after that I had trouble deciding whether I had liked him or not. I still have trouble, but I think I understand him better now. It always surprises me to think that I am now older than my father ever was. Did you like your father?''

The mother turned her head fully to the daughter now, definitely curious about the answer.

"I don't think so,'' said the girl. "No . . . I did like him . . . I . . .''

She was almost on the verge of tears, and Rostnikov pushed her a little further, unsure of whether he was doing it primarily for her therapy or to break through to conversation quickly, for once Karpo and Tkach came the approach would have to change and time might be lost. Rostnikov chewed at his lower lip and turned around to look down at the corpse.

"To tell the truth," he said. "For years I felt guilty about not liking my father. It was only after I became a man that I began to feel sorry for that fourteen-year-old boy who carried all that guilt for something that was not his fault. I felt better about my father after that."

He kept his back turned to the two women, but he could hear the sound of sobs suppressed, a spurt and then the gentle cry of grief. He had not wanted hysteria and had done his best to avoid it and had succeeded. He rose slowly and took off his coat. There were many questions, many things to do. He felt terrible, he felt wonderful. He felt the excitement of the chase and the inevitable curiosity at his lack of regret over the victim. He almost wished that it would not turn out to be too simple. Before it was over, Rostnikov would remember that wish and regret it.

CHAPTER THREE

"So," Rostnikov said, "who would want to do such a terrible thing?" He looked back over his shoulder to see if he would get a response, would break through the sobbing. If not, he would try again. It sometimes happened, actually more times than it did not, that a close friend, a neighbor, a relative committed a murder and those around indeed knew and could provide the name immediately. Rostnikov sensed that it would not be that simple, but not to try would be an error that might come back to haunt him.

Sonya Granovsky held her daughter and turned cold eyes on the pacing policeman.

"You," she said. "You killed him. One of you came in here and killed him, killed him for what he thought, what he said, what he wanted."

Grief had made the woman speak out in a way she would never have spoken in a natural state. It was refreshing and somewhat astonishing for Rostnikov to hear such outcries, and he secretly enjoyed moments of honesty, though he hid his pleasure behind a patient nod and sigh. In most cases, Russians had learned to control their outrage or kill it. Complaints were fruitless and could be dangerous.

"I did not kill your husband," he said softly.

"Not you, one of you, K.G.B.," she shouted. "They were following him, threatening him."

"No," said Rostnikov, wondering if he could ask for a cup of tea, not to keep the woman busy but to have something to do with his hands that wanted to touch objects in the room, the small painting on the wall, or to reach out and engulf the two thin women, to comfort and quiet them.

"No," he repeated. "Listen, it is not beyond the power of the state to act, but like this? No point. It is not . . ."

"Clean?" she finished, her body shaking.

"Clean, a good word," Rostnikov agreed.

"You did it," she repeated, turning her eyes back to the corpse. "That is what happened, what we will say, what I know. You can kill us, beat us, send us to the Vladimirka prison, but that is what we will say, what we know."

Rostnikov had seen this look before. He had lost for the moment. She had fixed on the idea, grasped it like a god, a cause, something to exist or be martyred for. She would, at least for now, cling to the belief that her husband had been killed by the state. The three, detective, woman, and girl, all looked at the body. A spot of blood had grown larger, seeping through the sheet. It spread in an uneven pattern, as if it had life, were groping. It cast a spell broken by a knock at the door.

Officer Drubkova opened the door and stood back to let Karpo and Tkach in. Karpo the Tatar looked first at Rostnikov, whose look told him how to act. Tkach looked first at the corpse, then at the two women and finally at Rostnikov, who made a nod to draw the two men closer.

"Officer Drubkova," Rostnikov whispered loud enough for everyone to hear, "will you please take Mrs. Granovsky and her daughter . . ." and he was at a loss as to where they could go. They certainly couldn't sit there watching the corpse. "Mrs. Granovsky, do you have someplace you can stay, someplace—"

"Our place is here," she spat back.

"You can hate me just as well in another apartment," he countered.

"No," she said between her teeth, "it is easier here."

"Perhaps you are right," Rostnikov agreed, "but I can't have it. We have work to do, a murderer to find. We can take you to a cell."

"Fine," said Sonya Granovsky, straightening her back and indeed, it would be fine with her. Rostnikov knew he had made a mistake.

"Why don't I take them someplace and question them?" Karpo said, turning his eyes on the two women. Sonya Granovsky looked up at the gaunt, almost corpse-like figure and suppressed a shudder.

"My brother, Kolya, he lives near," she said, "he might . . ."

"He will," Rostnikov added emphatically. "Officer Drubkova will see that you get there."

Drubkova moved quickly to the two women and helped them up with more gentleness than Rostnikov had thought she possessed. The girl was still crying softly as Officer Drubkova helped her put her coat on. Sonya Granovsky dressed herself and turned to face Rostnikov once more at the door. Her hat was on an angle, a comic angle like Popov the Clown. Maybe with a wisp of hair in her eyes she would look like the dissheveled American actress whose name he couldn't remember.

"I meant what I said," she said with a tremor.

Rostnikov nodded and watched Drubkova lead the two figures out.

"Drubkova," he called when the door was almost shut and the woman hurried back into the room. "You, personally, are to remain with them all night. If they don't let you stay in the apartment, remain outside as close as you can. Hear what you can hear and prepare a report. You will be relieved in the morning. Tkach, see to it."

Tkach nodded and Drubkova left, her brown uniform tight with pride.

When the door closed, Rostnikov went to the sofa and sat heavily in it. Karpo knelt by the body and pulled back the sheet.

"Tkach, go out in the hall and tell the man out there to have the evidence people get up here now." Tkach did as he was told and Rostnikov watched Karpo examine the body.

"You frightened that poor grieving widow," Rostnikov said with a smile.

"A talent developed over the years," Karpo

answered, looking into the eyes of the corpse.

"And what does my corpse tell you?" Rostnikov asked.

"Secrets," said Karpo softly. "He whispers to me. The dead and I get along quite well."

"Better than the living?" said Rostnikov, watching the Tatar's fingers explore the area around the wound.

"Yes," said Karpo evenly. "Whoever did this had strength. This sickle is old and rusty, yet the penetration is deep and through a bone. A strong man."

"Or a madman or woman given the strength of purpose or anger," Rostnikov said, looking at the dead man's face. It was an angry face even in death. He would be forever angry.

Karpo rose.

"Assuming he was not lying down when he was struck," Karpo began.

"He was not," said Rostnikov. "The trail of blood is from the front door."

"Of course," Karpo continued. "The killer was not tall, the wound indicates someone no bigger than . . ."

". . . me," Rostnikov finished.

Karpo shrugged and Tkach reentered the room. "And what are you working on?" Rostnikov asked the young man. "Just the most important cases."

"State liquor store thefts," he answered quickly. "Someone is breaking into state liquor stores at night. Huge amounts have been taken. It is a very large, very bold black market operation. I have—"

"No details," Rostnikov said holding up a hand and looking back at the corpse. "That will wait. You get two, maybe three hours sleep and then start following up on Granovsky's friends. Be nice, be kind, be sympathetic. Find out if he had enemies, what they think. Be discreet, but find out.''

''Shall I take a uniformed man with me?'' Tkach asked.

''What you think best,'' responded Rostnikov, without turning around. ''Would you see if there is any tea here?''

''Yes,'' said Tkach moving past the corpse and to the kitchen area. ''You think the tea . . .''

''I'd like some tea,'' Rostnikov closed. ''Don't worry about fingerprints. The killer didn't come in and make tea. He or she did it and ran. There was a K.G.B. man watching the place when Granovsky was murdered.''

''That is Granovsky, the . . .'' Tkach said turning from his search to take another look at the corpse.

''It is,'' said Rostnikov looking at Karpo, whose face betrayed nothing. ''And you Emil, your cases?''

''Apartment robberies, assault, and someone masquerading as a police officer has been preying on African students at Moscow University, pretending to suspect them of crimes, taking their money. Complaints . . .''

''Ah,'' sighed Rostnikov, listening for the sound of boiling water, ''political.''

''Everything is political,'' Karpo added, wandering to the window to examine the hole.

''I sit corrected,'' Rostnikov.

''I was not correcting you,'' said Karpo. ''I was observing.''

"Yes," sighed Rostnikov, rising with effort to the sound of a knock at the door. "Well this is more political. When the evidence people finish, I want you to take that sickle and find what you can find."

The door opened and three dark figures entered slowly. One held a suitcase, another, wearing thick, tinted glasses, carried a camera.

"Tkach, we are leaving," said Rostnikov. "Gentlemen, there will be hot water in a few minutes for tea."

The third dark figure, who wore no glasses and carried nothing, spoke in a rumbling voice that sounded like a Metro train.

"You had a message from Procurator Timofeyeva," he said. "A taxi driver was killed a little while ago, two witnesses. Before he died, the taxi driver said, 'Granovsky!'"

"Karpo," Rostnikov said pulling his coat on, "you take that. I will pay a visit to the K.G.B. in the morning and we will meet at Petrovka . . . when we can meet at Petrovka."

The trio of dark figures moved past Rostnikov, who turned for a last look at Granovsky—an angry man and look what his anger got him. There was perhaps a lesson in this room, on that face. Rostnikov absorbed the lesson without thinking about it.

"Do any of you remember the name of the American movie actress with the yellow hair that kept falling in her face?" Rostnikov asked. "She had to keep blowing it out of her eyes."

"Veronska Lake," said the man with the bag, moving to the corpse.

"No," sighed Rostnikov scratching his ear, "the

hair wasn't designed to be over the eyes. It was always by accident.''

"I see," said the man with the thick dark glasses, groping his way to the kitchen in search of the tea.

"Maybe it was Deanna Durbin?" said the man with the camera.

"No," said Rostnikov, "thanks." It was one of those annoying things of no consequence that would drive you mad if you couldn't remember. There was a chance, not much of a chance perhaps, but a chance that Rostnikov's career might be in danger, but this nearly forgotten American movie star had cropped up and had to be named to set his mind at rest. It would come, it would come.

An hour later Emil Karpo entered the M.V.D. building on Petrovka Street. The armed duty guard looked at him with no sign of recognition but made no move to stop him. The older officer at the desk, fully uniformed, white-haired, involuntarily nodded in greeting at the striding Karpo, though he knew Karpo was not one to respond to social gestures.

A dark suited man named Klishkov passed Karpo on the way down. Klishkov who bore an ugly red scar across his face and nose from an attack by a drunk, glanced at Karpo, who let his eyes respond in unblinking acknowledgement.

The door to Room 312 was closed but a light was on behind it. It was one of many "discussion" rooms in Petrovka. Such rooms could be used for meetings, conspiracies, or interviews with suspects or witnesses. Because of the uneven heating of the building, some of the interview rooms were painfully cold in the winter while others were oppressively hot. This was a cold one. Karpo opened the door and faced two men across the small table in the center of the room. The Roshkovs, father and son, were startled and started to rise. Karpo ignored them and turned to the uniformed officer who stood in the corner. The officer, well aware of Karpo's reputation, moved smartly forward and handed him a clipboard with a report attached. Karpo took it and read it ignoring the sudden babbling of Vladimir, the elder Roshkov.

"We've done nothing," pleaded the old man, "nothing." His eyes, yellow and soft, were moist with self-pity.

Karpo handed the report back to the officer and faced the old man. The sudden attention caught the old man in mid-sentence, stopping him. There was something about this corpse-like policeman that made such rambling pathetic even to Vladimir Roshkov, who had spent an eighty-year lifetime perfecting it, but the pause was only that. Vladimir Roshkov could no more hold his tongue than he could join the Bolshoi Ballet.

"Officer, sir," he pleaded, actually bringing his hands together, "we did nothing. We were on our way to work, to work. There is no crime in going to work, is there sir, comrade, officer?"

Karpo said nothing but turned his eyes on Pytor Roshkov who sat sullen, a coarse brown police blanket wrapped around his legs.

"Are you ill?" Karpo asked.

"No," said Pytor, "I have no pants. That cab tore off my pants, and the police wouldn't let me go home

47

for another pair. Mind you, I'm not complaining. I understand, but . . . I understand.''

"My son is not complaining at all,'' shouted the old man, rapping his son on the head. "He's happy to help any way he can. We both are, but we had nothing to do . . .''

"Sit,'' commanded Karpo, and the old man sat next to his son, his voice momentarily stilled but his mouth was open and ready, his teeth poor and jagged.

"You saw the man get out of the cab?'' Karpo said, standing with his hands behind his back over the two men.

"Yes,'' said the old man, "he was all in black, a madman. I thought he was going to kill us. His clothes were good, not new. My first thought was, 'Here is some capitalist tourist drunk and up to no good.' ''

"He was a foreigner?'' tried Karpo.

"Yes,'' went on the old man, "definitely a foreigner, English or American, he . . .''

"Did he speak?'' tried Karpo.

"I . . . I . . . ,'' stammered the old man, anxious to please.

"No,'' said the son, hugging the blanket over his vulnerable legs. "He said nothing. He just ran down Petro Street.'' Pytor Roshkov had decided to fix his eyes on the fascinating painting on the wall of the first meeting of the Presidium.

"Then you don't know if he was a foreigner,'' Karpo continued.

"No,'' said the son.

"Yes,'' said the father.

"If you would try less hard to please me and harder to

48

simply tell the truth, you will get out of here much faster and back to your home or work," Karpo said. "However, if you continue like this, it may take hours before we feel we can let you go. Now, can you describe the man you saw running from the cab on Petro Street?"

"I . . . ," began old Roshkov and stopped, clamping his jaw tight with an audible click.

"No," said the son. "He was a regular man in a black coat and hat and he was young, at least he was fast like a young man."

"And you heard Ivan Sharikov say 'Granovsky'?" asked Karpo.

"We don't know any Ivan Sharikov," wept the old man. "We are just shopkeepers. We aren't political, just poor peasants who . . ."

"Sharikov was the taxi driver who was murdered," Karpo said evenly.

"Granovsky," said Pytor, moving his eyes from the painting to look at Karpo, but unable to hold the look.

"So," babbled the old man, "it's simple. You find this man Granovsky who killed the cab driver, and everything is fine. So simple. How many Granovsky's can there be in Moscow? Our police can find him like that."

"Old man, you are babbling with guilt," Karpo said softly, wanting to shake the trembling creature into simple responses. "I don't care what you have done. I want information."

"Done?" said the old man, rising and pointing a thick finger at his chest. "Done? We have done nothing, nothing. If you mean those shoes, well, those shoes. How were we to know the soles were cardboard.

We bought them from . . ."

"Father, shut up," shouted the suddenly frantic son rising to quiet the old man and letting the blanket drop to the floor.

"But . . ." continued the old man, prepared to confess to seven decades of crime. The naked son clasped a hand over the old man's mouth and Karpo glanced at the uniformed officer who was trying to control a grin.

"Get them out," said Karpo.

"We want to help," said the old man, leaning forward on the table as his son retrieved his blanket.

Karpo left the room, feeling the aura of a coming headache. He would retrieve the sickle from the evidence men and work on that. The sickle would be tangible and might say much without speaking. A pinpoint of irritation vibrated somewhere in Karpo's brain, and he thought of Rostnikov's question about the American actress. A voice wanted to ask Karpo how anything could be accomplished in such emotionalism, irrelevance, and chaos, but he stilled the voice before it could speak and remembered Rostnikov's past successes and reminded himself that the Roshkovs were a step in the movement toward an ideal Soviet state, a movement which he knew would not be an easy one.

Perhaps the room was not getting larger. It was a thought he had never considered and the voice of his father had never suggested. This thought came in something like the voice of the cab driver he had killed, the cab driver with the bloody face, the gross pig of a cab driver to whom he owed so much. The smashing of the vodka bottle. The moisture of the vodka in his face. The feeling of solidity when he plunged the bottle into the fat surprised face. The two men in the snow. It had been a warning to stay alert.

He sat on the floor of the apartment, his coat still on, the darkness surrounding him. As the minutes passed, the light from the single window illuminated the familiar room, but it looked unfamiliar, new to him. The world had changed. And then the room had threatened to grow. He had scrambled from the floor to the old chest of drawers, his parent's old chest and had pulled out the heavy hammer. The handle had been made on the farm by his father and the heavy iron head purchased before he was born. It felt solid, good, and cool. He let the metal head cool his burning cheek and forehead, but the room threatened to grow and he thought again that the room might not be getting larger. What if he were growing smaller? The thought made him shriek and shiver. There should be someone to help. He should turn the lights on, but he couldn't move. He wanted to put the idea away but it was fascinating. Maybe he would just keep getting smaller and smaller and when she came in in the morning after work, she would step on him, squash him like a bug. There would be a small spot of blood on the floor and she would make a sandwich and go to bed, not knowing what she had done.

But he knew what she had done. Granovsky was smart, so smart, but he was no more and there was no heaven or hell for him. Now he, sitting there with the hammer, was in control of the world. He could kill a cab driver to verify his experience. He was not growing smaller. The room was not getting bigger. It had always passed before and would pass again. He would sit, covered with a terrible sweat, and he would feel fear and no one would help him. She had promised to help him, to stay near him, but that had been a lie. He had only the voice of his father and victims and the hammer. He cuddled the hammer, placed it under his arm, put it between his legs like a wooden erection and laughed. He had taken charge of the world. There would be no more fear or listening to others or standing in line. She would find out. She had changed all this and would get her reward, and the reward would be the hammer as Granovsky's reward had been the sickle. There should be something beyond that, something to do. Others to be shown, taught. It would come. He knew it would come. He thought of one of his mother's meals of sausages and dumplings and cheese and the thought held at bay the growing of the room,

CHAPTER FOUR

The file on Aleksander Granovsky had been thick and neat. Sasha Tkach expected as much and knew that the K.G.B. must have drawers of files on Granovsky, but they were files he could not hope to get or see. He had taken the file to the large office room where he had shared a desk with another junior inspector named Zelach. The bottom drawer was supposed to be Sasha's for records, storing tea, but Zelach kept infringing on the space with his own things. Sasha did not mind sharing the drawer. He minded Zelach's sandwiches, which left a garlic smell on all of Sasha's notes and papers.

The lights in the large room were dim, and one or two other inspectors were working. Sasha thought he heard the grunt of a greeting from Klishkov, but he couldn't be sure. The room was, even when full, a quiet place in spite of the twenty or thirty people who rambled in it at any given time. If one had to shout at a suspect or underling, one was expected to move to an investigating room. The room was also clean, almost antiseptic. One could never go back into the garbage to retrieve an inadvertently discarded note.

Sasha had compiled a list of Granovsky's acquaintances. The compiling had not taken long, perhaps an hour, even with corresponding addresses, but it was a bit too early to begin to act. There was nothing wrong with questioning people at four in the morning, but Rostnikov had told him to be friendly and persuasive rather than demanding. It was an easier order to give than to execute, for Sasha knew from experience that his youth and disarmingly innocent face would not carry him far in most investigations. Muscovites were too cautious. Innocence was something they distrusted in anyone and were particularly wary of in a policeman.

Sasha pulled out his lunch and began to eat it at his desk, after looking across the room to see if the other officers were interested in his activities. Inspectors were not supposed to eat at their desks. They were supposed to go to the building cafeteria. By pretending to reach for files in his drawer, Sasha managed to sneak bites of the sandwich and wonder if he had enough money to stop at a *Stolovaya* for lunch or some *borshcht* and a sausage.

The door opened across the room and Emil Karpo, looking like the angel of death searching for his next victim, strode in, carrying a sickle. Sasha sat up with a mouthful of sandwich, and Karpo glanced in his direction. Sasha nodded, trying to hide his bite of sandwich with a gulp that sent him into a choking gasp. Karpo paid no attention and moved to his own desk, where he placed the sickle gently in front of him and closed his eyes.

By six, Sasha Tkach had had enough waiting. He had memorized the list of twelve names but not the addresses. He placed the list carefully in his pocket, put on his coat and hat and strode out of the office past Karpo who sat with closed eyes over the sickle. Karpo looked like a man with a headache, but Sasha knew it was more likely that he was simply deep in thought. He did not pause to ask. Like the other younger inspectors he had a fearful respect for Karpo who was known to act with cold fury in the face of violence. The younger men were afraid that they might be teamed with the Tatar one of the times he risked his life and possibly theirs.

It was a cold dark morning promising nothing, but Sasha Tkach asked much of it as he hurried down the steps and towards the first friend of Aleksander Granovsky.

Not far from the Kremlin is one of the busiest intersections in Moscow, Dzerzhinsky Square, where as many as half a million people come each day. Many of them come to visit the Museum of History and Reconstruction of Moscow or the Mayakovsky Museum. Others come to the Slavyansky Bazar Restaurant or the Berlin Hotel, but most come to two massive buildings. One building is the Detsky Mir or Children's World, the biggest children's store in Russia. The other building is a strange, hulking creature in two sections at the corner of Kirov and Dzerzhinsky Streets. One half of the building pre-dates the Revolution. The other half was completed in 1948, using the labor of captured German soldiers. When the project was completed, the German soldiers were reportedly executed so that they could not divulge information about the labyrinth of rooms they had built. The building does not show up on the official tourist books and pictures of the square. Most such pictures or drawings are presented from the point of view of this massive building, the Lubyanka, which houses the K.G.B.

The square itself is named in honor of the man whose tall bronze statue stands in the center of the intersection, seemingly guarding the building. Felix Dzerzhinsky, who died in 1926, is described by those same guide books as an eminent Party leader, a Soviet statesman, and a close comrade of Lenin. He was, in addition, the principal draftsman of what became the Soviet secret police. The proximity of statue and building is not coincidental.

Until the late 1950s, the organization which became the K.G.B. contented itself with political matters and allowed the regular police to go its own way in dealing with other crimes. The K.G.B. had bided its time after the liquidation of Lavrenti Beria who was executed by the others vying with him for power, Malenkov, Khrushchev, and Molotov. Beria had built a career by kissing Stalin's hand in public and tearing arms out of sockets like the petals of a flower. When he died, the K.G.B. adopted a posture of extreme patriotism and disinterest in the petty disagreements of man—including murder. With a rash of black market crimes and capitalistic enterprises at the end of the 1950s, the K.G.B. tested its strength by asserting control over economic crimes. Since all crimes can be viewed as political and economic, the K.G.B. could take over whatever crime it chose to investigate.

This knowledge was clear to Porfiry Rostnikov as he sat waiting on the wooden bench at K.G.B. headquarters. He had been in the building several times in the past and had noticed how quiet it was. People spoke in whispers as if in a place of worship. Even the typewriters and phones seemed to be muted. Dark wood dominated railings, benches, ceilings. Rostnikov thought it needed only religious icons, a few saints sprinkled here and there, but the K.G.B. was most careful not to elevate any secular political saints.

Rostnikov had arrived by metro at 6:30 after a few hours of non-sleep in his bed trying to rest, thinking and not thinking. A dream came in which he had to eat a sausage pudding with a heavy iron hammer. Comrade Timofeyeva urged him on with quotations from Lenin, but he made a mess of it, trying to keep from getting his coat dirty. To get a coat cleaned in Moscow was a major effort. Finally, in the dream he had grown angry, had lifted the hammer over his head, to establish a new U.S.S.R. record for a hammer lift, and brought it down heavily on the dish, sending pudding, sausage, and shards of plate in all directions. He had awakened with a grunt and said, "Carole Lombard."

"What?" his wife had asked dreamily.

"Carole Lombard," Rostnikov grunted straining to see the time on his clock. "An American movie actress whose hair kept falling in her face in some movie."

"That was your dream?" asked his wife turning to him.

"No," he had said, sitting up to find his trousers again. "I don't know why it came to me. Perhaps to clear my mind."

"Be sure to eat," she had replied, turning over for another hour or two of sleep.

He had grunted again, slipped on his pants, washed,

and shaved after boiling some water for the task and then spent fifteen minutes with the weights. Only with the weights could he step outside of himself and watch. Once he began, it was as if he had no real part of it, that he was just an observer. The exercise of will was not to do more or to conquer the pain of adding weight. Oh no, for Rostnikov the problem was to stop, to feel. It was too easy to simply sink into a state of forgetfulness and go on forever observing himself lift and add weights. The addition of weight had, indeed, proved a problem, but not a psychological one. It was simply hard to get weights in Moscow. He had tried improvising, but the balance was impossible. Finally, he had turned to the black market—a storekeeper he had once decided not to bring in for a minor infraction knew a man who knew a woman who knew an athlete who could get weights. There was an annual competition for men and women fifty and over in Sokolniki Recreation Park in June. Rostnikov had decided to enter and was, though he had told no one, not even himself, in training. He went over events, calculated weights, and worried about his leg.

"Inspector Rostnikov."

Rostnikov looked up. He had been aware of the black suited man moving toward him, but he had been trying to decide whether to try to buy a new weight bar.

"Yes," Rostnikov answered.

"Follow me," said the man. Rostnikov rose and followed. His leg slowed him down, but he managed to keep up with the straight-backed man with curly brown hair down the corridor and up a short stairway. The man made it clear that they were not walking together, that he was a guide and not a new acquaintance. They stopped at a door without name or number, and the guide knocked once, firmly.

"In," came a man's raspy voice, and the guide opened the door, stepped back and let Rostnikov move past him. The guide left, closing the door behind him, and Rostnikov found himself in an office in sharp contrast to that of Comrade Timofeyeva. This office was carpeted, a dark brown carpet, not too thick, but carpet nonetheless. The posters on the wall were familiar ones from Rostnikov's boyhood, colorfully urging productivity and solidarity, posters with bright reds and firm faces. Each was framed. The furniture was comfortable, chairs with arms and dark nylon padded seats, and the desk itself was well polished and old, probably an antique from before the Revolution. The man behind the desk was thin, his face dark with the memory of some labors in youth. His hair was white and well groomed. He wore a dark suit and blue tie.

"I am Colonel Drozhkin," he said, extending an open calloused palm toward the chair on the other side of the desk. Colonel Drozhkin's accent was that of a workingman, a holdover peasant. It had probably taken him some effort to retain it in what must have been years in Moscow. Rostnikov sat and Drozhkin did the same, a thin reed of anticipation behind the huge desk, which his fingers touched possessively and nervously.

"I'm sorry to have kept you waiting," Drozhkin said moving some papers on his desk and making it quite clear that he was not sorry at all. The waiting and the tone made it clear who was master and who servant in this situation of comrades.

"I understand," said Rostnikov, and indeed he did.

"Good," said Drozhkin, "yes, good. Now you are here in relation to the murder of Aleksander Granovsky. I assume you want some cooperation, ideas, eh?"

"That would be most appreciated," Rostnikov replied.

"Yes, of course, we will do what we can, but it is you who must find this madman and find him quickly. It is best if we have no direct part in the investigation if at all possible. You understand?"

"Fully," replied Rostnikov.

"Good, then what . . . ?" said Drozhkin holding up his hands.

"You were watching Granovsky," Rostnikov plunged in, looking directly at the K.G.B. Colonel. You had a man on him last night, a man who may be able to tell me something if I could talk to him."

Drozhkin's wrinkled, worn face tightened, his jaw moved forward and Rostnikov knew that it would not be pleasant to be questioned by Colonel Drozhkin.

"We were not there to protect him," the colonel said, returning Rostnikov's gaze.

"Of course not," Rostnikov said sincerely.

"And we were not there to harm him," the little colonel went on emphatically. "Nothing could look worse, would be worse than . . . Perhaps you wouldn't understand. It would not be good, is not good for us that this happened."

"Then," went on Rostnikov, "it would be best if I could talk to your man and get on with catching this murderer as quickly as possible. He has murdered a second time and may be about to do so again."

"I know," sighed Drozhkin with a wave of his hand. "That is not my concern or interest. I don't know if I can let you talk to the man you wish to speak to." Drozhkin eyed Rostnikov, who did not answer and went on. "Is there something you have to say further to change my mind?"

Rostnikov looked down at his hands and had the urge to ask this tense K.G.B. man to compare callouses and lives, but instead he said, "May I be frank?"

A tick of a smile touched the older man's face and hid again.

"Is that ever wise?" he said, leaning back.

Rostnikov shrugged and shifted his weight before responding. He did not really mean to be frank, and both men knew it.

"I have a task, a murderer to catch and not much time to do it. Wisdom may have to be tempered with expediency. I think you planned to let me talk to your man from the moment I walked into this building or I would not be here."

Drozhkin stood up quickly, held a comment, and turned to speak to the wall.

"It wasn't wise, but I see your point," he said.

"Thank you, colonel."

The colonel turned, in control once more, looking down at the police officer.

Drozhkin moved to one of the posters on the wall, his back still to his visitor, and straightened it, though it needed no straightening. The poster was of a hefty woman with a shovel, looking over her shoulder to urge on her fellows, who had no space in the picture.

"I have your file, Inspector Rostnikov," said the

colonel, stepping back to assess the job he had done in lining up the poster.

"Of course," answered Rostnikov, realizing that any answer was treading dangerous ground.

"For many reasons, you are lucky to have the job and responsibility which you have," said the colonel, turning once more to face the policeman.

"True of all of us who are fortunate enough to serve the state," said Rostnikov folding his hands on his coat. The colonel's remark could have meant many things from the black market weights to the fact that Rostnikov's wife was Jewish, but the point was clear again.

"Then we understand each other," Drozhkin repeated.

"Fully," answered Rostnikov, wondering how long this would continue, whether the colonel would simply keep him here for days going in verbal circles. It was probably a habit of the old man's, a habit of interrogation which he could not break.

Drozhkin moved swiftly and silently across the brown carpet to his desk and picked up the phone.

"Zhenya, get Khrapenko, send him to the interrogation room on one. Tell him he is to be interviewed by a police inspector and is to tell him everything he wants to know about last night. Yes, now." He replaced the black phone firmly and looked at Rostnikov.

"You are to confine your questions to last night and deal only with the particulars of your investigation," said the colonel.

It struck Rostnikov for the first time that the colonel himself must have someone above him to whom he would have to report, and the situation was perhaps as dangerous for the old man as it was for the police officer.

"Of course," said Rostnikov amiably. "In fact, I would like, if possible, to have the . . ."

"Interview," Drozhkin completed.

"Yes," Rostnikov went on, "the interview. I would like it recorded so that you can hear it."

"It will be," said the colonel, sitting behind the desk and examining the policeman once again. "You knew it would be. Don't play the fool."

Rostnikov shrugged.

"Have you ever been to Kiev?" the colonel asked suddenly, and Rostnikov was bewildered for the first time since entering the room. He tried to protect himself from whatever it was that was coming.

"My son is . . ."

"I know, I know that," said the colonel with irritation, "I am not asking a political question."

"Once," said Rostnikov, shifting uncomfortably, "I had to deliver a prisoner years ago."

"Did you see the interior of the Cathedral of St. Sofiya?"

"No, I did not."

"Decadent, yes," sighed the colonel, "but beautiful. The chandeliers, the recreation of the byzantine. It is without meaning, the epitome of what could be accomplished by medieval princes, a reminder of the temptation of the impractical, a reminder that we must remain strong. I have gone to that church many times to feel the temptation to fight it, to emerge strong again. Do you have such a place, comrade inspector?"

Rostnikov shrugged. "In my head, perhaps, like most Russians."

Drozhkin moved from behind the desk and motioned for Rostnikov to rise. He placed a hand on the policeman's shoulder and guided him toward the door.

"Return to that place now, inspector, and draw strength from it. Meet the challenge, or those with stronger wills will have to take your place."

"Of course," sighed Rostnikov, "that is the strength of socialism. If one falls, you or I, there is someone right behind to take up the task."

A knock at the door interrupted the conversation, and the man who had led Rostnikov to the room stepped in.

"Zhenya, take Inspector Rostnikov to the interrogation room. He is to be given fifteen minutes to talk to Khrapenko. Understood?"

"Yes," replied Zhenya.

"And you, inspector," the old man said in his heavy accent, "are to take no notes and make no reference to this interview in any trial that might take place without my direct permission."

"And in your absence?" Rostnikov asked innocently.

"To whomever occupies this office. You walk dangerously, comrade," Drozhkin said between clenched teeth.

"I don't mean to," said Rostnikov. "I simply wish to get my job done."

"As do we all." Drozhkin moved back to his desk, and Zhenya stepped into the hall with Rostnikov behind him. Rostnikov reached back to close the door, but the voice of the old man inside stopped him.

"Now that we are friends," Drozhkin said with a touch of irony that sent a chill through Rostnikov, "I think I can give you some confidential news. Your son's brigade has been sent to Afghanistan. That is confidential information. I thought you would be proud and happy to know."

"Yes, I am, and I thank you for your thoughts and consideration, comrade," Rostnikov managed to get out as he closed the door behind him.

As he limped after the rapidly moving Zhenya, the news struck him like blows from steel weight bars. Iosef was in a place where Russian soldiers were being killed. Visions of his own war, of death, of Rostov, sliced through Rostnikov, and fear for his son brought burning moisture to his armpits. But he also thought, at one level of consciousness, that Colonel Drozhkin had seemed overly concerned, responsible, and emotional; that he had invested a great deal in this case of Aleksander Granovsky. The colonel had said too much. True, he had provoked Rostnikov to intemperate statement, but he, himself, had been as guilty. Age, responsibility, concern over possible blame for Granovsky's death or at least of negligence might account for it, but a K.G.B. man of Drozhkin's age should surely have learned to control himself, to weather many crises.

Zhenya stopped before a door and Rostnikov hurried to catch up.

"Fifteen minutes," Zhenya said.

"Fifteen minutes," Rostnikov agreed.

The room was small and bare. Khrapenko, young and nervous-looking, was pacing the floor. He stopped as Rostnikov entered, tried to pull himself together and, before the policeman could speak, said, "I am Khrapenko."

And, thought a puzzled Rostnikov, you look very close to being a fool, which means there will be two of them in this room for fifteen minutes.

CHAPTER FIVE

Though there are rules and regulations, restrictions and requirements, it is no easier in Moscow to find a killer or a saint than it is in New York, Tokyo, or Rome. If the world does not know this, the police do, and so they learn to value patience and good shoes.

Sasha Tkach had begun his day and was putting his patience to practice.

He was sitting in a small, surprisingly warm room drinking a cup of tea. He had lost the opportunity to remove his coat, and he had lost the initiative in the conversation when the man to whom he was speaking, Simon Lvov, had greeted him warmly, invited him in and offered him tea. Lvov was a tall man of seventy-five who stooped over slightly and smoked a pipe. His dark grey hair was unkempt, and perched on his huge nose were the glasses all too familiar to Russians, the standard dark, round frames like those of the American comedian Harold Lloyd. Tkach had been prepared for hostility, trickery, deception, but not for this warm man in a dark cardigan sweater who ushered him in and made him sit in a soft, ancient chair.

"You are a young man," Lvov said, simply, in reply to Tkach's first question about Granovsky. It was clear that, from some source, Lvov had heard about Granovsky's death. It was also clear that he was not in a state of deep mourning. According to the information Tkach had, this Lvov had been a scientist—an agronomist or something; he was one of Moscow's leading dissidents and had worked closely with the murdered Granovsky. Yet for a scientist he was maddeningly indirect.

Before long Tkach had completely lost control of the interview, and Lvov, sitting comfortably at a small table, leaned forward on his elbows and watched the puffs of smoke from his pipe while he told a parable.

"Once there was a powerful warden in a prison in another country, let us call that country Peru, shall we?"

"Yes," agreed Tkach, sipping his tea and assuming he was watching the first of stages of the man's senility. "Peru."

"Well," Lvov continued, "a friend of mine had the misfortune to find himself in that prison, and one night the warden had my friend brought into a large room filled with guards and newspaper reporters. It was very late at night and my friend, in prison for counter-revolutionary activity, had been sleeping. He rubbed his eyes at the huge gathering and rubbed them again when he saw that the fat warden wore a rare smile under his great mustache. The warden ordered my friend to a table in the center of the room on which stood, or rather slumped, a black cloth bag. The conversation in the room stopped, and the warden cleared his throat.

" 'An anmesty has been called for all political prisoners in honor of the one hundreth anniversary of liberation day,' said the warden with a sweep of his hand. 'However, since this prison contains only the worst and most dangerous elements, our president is reluctant to include you and your fellows. But our president is a fair man and in public display he has ordered me to give you an even chance to secure liberation for yourself and the others who plotted against the state. In that bag are two small white balls. On one ball is written "freedom" and on the other "prison." You will, by virtue of your high rank in the counter-revolutionary conspiracy, place your hand in that bag and remove one of the balls. If the ball contains the word "freedom," you all go free. If it contains the word "prison," then you all remain. The press has been invited to prove that we abide by our word. Now take out a ball and let us see what your fate is.'

"Do you see my friend's dilemma, Officer . . . ?"

"Lvov, no, I . . ." said Tkach, suddenly needing very much to urinate.

"My friend was no fool," Lvov went on, examining the bowl of his pipe. "He knew that the fat warden with the great mustache hated him, and what better way to get rid of an enemy in prison than to make him the object of hatred of his fellow inmates? Surely, my friend knew, if he selected the ball marked 'prison' the other prisoners would hear of it, be told of it, and he knew there were those among the prisoners whose minds had been eroded by brutality and who might very well kill my friend for his ill luck and theirs. My friend pretended to still be sleepy as his mind worked rapidly. There is no chance of pulling the right ball, he thought. The warden would not look so confident with an even chance of losing his pets.

"'The truth was obvious to my friend. Both balls have the word 'prison,' and it made no difference which one he picked. No one would dare challenge the powerful warden by asking to see the remaining ball, least of all my friend, who knew that any effort to do so would surely result in his own death. But remember, my friend was a clever man and he made up his mind quickly.

"He strode to the table, plunged his hand into the bag, grabbed a ball, and without looking at it, threw it into his mouth and swallowed it in one gulp, almost choking. A gasp rose from the crowd, and the warden reached for his pistol.

" 'What are you trying to do?' shouted the purple-faced little man. 'Nothing,' answered my friend innocently, pretending a combination of stupidity and drowsiness. 'I thought I was supposed to eat it. Anyway, there is no harm done. All you have to do is see which ball remains in the bag and the one I ate is, by elimination, the other one.' More tea Inspector Tkach?"

"Officer Tkach," Tkach corrected. "No thank you, but if . . ."

"Well," continued Lvov, examining the bowl of his pipe, "A sharp-featured young reporter standing near my friend shouted, 'Ridiculous. Ridiculous, but true.' A murmur of approval ran through the reporters, who were anxious to discover the fate of the prisoners. The warden, teeth clenched and eyes magnificent with hatred fixed on my friend, dumped the ball onto the table and it bounced, bounced, bounced toward the sharp-featured young reporter who snatched it and read it.

" 'Freedom,' said the reporter handing the ball to the warden. 'This ball says "freedom." He swallowed the ball that said "prison." ' In seconds the room was clear, and my friend was surrounded by guards and faced by the evil warden. Several weeks later my friend was found dead; someone had stabbed him with a—"

"Sickle," Tkach supplied.

Lvov pointed his pipe at the young detective and nodded, pushing his glasses back. "Yes, I think it was something like that. No one ever discovered whether he had been killed by guards or prisoners."

Lvov rose and stretched, trying to straighten up, but was refused that pleasure by his body.

"Outsmarted himself," said Tkach.

"No, oh no," Lvov said with a pained grin. "Not at all. He had been absolutely correct. Both balls had 'prison' marked on them. The sharp-featured reporter had used the opportunity to do a good turn for the powerful warden, who rewarded the reporter years later by having him imprisoned on some false charge. Then the young reporter told the truth, but it was too late to do my friend any good, and since the warden denied it, it did no good for the reporter or the remaining prisoners."

"That is indeed a sad tale," said Tkach, finishing his tea and forcing himself out of the comfortable chair. "Am I to gather from it that you will not cooperate in my investigation?"

Lvov shrugged. "I'd be happy to cooperate. I will

cooperate, but I am afraid there is nothing I can tell you. Nothing that would do Granovsky or me or you any good, nothing that would help, you see?''

"Help who?'' said Tkach.

"Who are we trying to help?'' Lvov countered.

"If you could answer me with an answer instead of a question or an evasion,'' Tkach answered irritably, "I could—''

"All right,'' Lvov answered, suddenly dropping his whimsy. "Who would it help?''

Tkach was confused. The answer seemed so obvious.

"We want to find the person who murdered Aleksander Granovsky,'' he answered reasonably. "Don't you?''

"That depends on who you find, doesn't it?''

"Whoever it is . . .'' Tkach began.

"If it is some poor madman, some enemy, will that bring Granovsky back?''

"More questions,'' sighed Tkach.

"Yes, and more. If it is the K.G.B., will they be tried?''

"I don't see . . .''

"That is right,'' sighed Lvov enormously, "you do not see. I have no answers for you, young man, only questions and parables. I'll tell you but one thing. Aleksander Granovsky was a perfect icon, a man who enjoyed the prospect of martyrdom and who enjoyed exercising power. He had few friends and many enemies. To know him was to dislike him. The government knew and feared him. The same was true of those who simply met him waiting in lines for tea.

Moscow is your suspect. You have interviewed one. You have but six or seven million left. I bid you good luck and good day."

Tkach's confusion was enormous, as was the call of his bladder. No one had ever spoken to him like this. Everyone feared the police.

"Would you rather I have you brought to Petrovka for questioning?" Tkach tried.

Lvov shrugged and smiled.

"If it pleases you," he said, filling his pipe and searching for a match. "You will get no more. The problem, young man, is that you can no longer threaten a man who has nothing to lose. I am old. I am sick and possibly dying. I am not permitted to work, and I have no family. What will you take from me, my pipe?" And with this question, Lvov threw the pipe against the wall. Pieces of tobacco rained out and Tkach watched the old man's shoulders sag.

He went out the door closing it softly behind him.

"The toilet is at the end of the hall," Lvov's voice came through the thin door.

It was slightly after noon when Tkach made his way back to Petrovka, which was alive with activity. People with briefcases hurried past, arguing. Dirty men in near rags being hurried along. Shouts heard through thick doors. A typical day for the police. The building restored Sasha Tkach's confidence, which had been shaken by his experience of the morning.

When Tkach entered the inspector's small office at the end of the large bustling room full of detectives, Rostnikov whispered, "Close the door behind you."

Karpo was sitting in one of the two chairs, holding the sickle in his hand. Tkach closed the door behind him and took off his coat, eager for information.

"Something's broken?" he asked.

"No," said Rostnikov. "I want to eat the pirozhki I bought on the way back." And with that, he pulled a brown paper bundle from his desk drawer and unwrapped it. "Would you care for some?"

Karpo didn't bother to respond. Tkach hesitated.

"Take it," sighed Rostnikov. "It's more than I should have."

Tkach took the sandwich and began to eat.

Karpo reported first. The sickle was a kind no longer manufactured, one made sixty years ago by a small company in Tula. Used by small farms. No fingerprints. Nothing.

Tkach, between bites, reported his failure with Lvov; he left out the parable, most of the verbal exchange and the information about his weak bladder. He also reported on similarly fruitless interviews with four other friends of Granovsky.

"One thing," Tkach added. "As much as they refused to talk, they felt compelled to tell how much they disliked Granovsky as a man. His enemies were not just political. I have eight more names on the primary list. If I exhaust that, perhaps I can get more leads."

There was little room to maneuver in the small office, and it had no sense of home or comfort. There were no pictures on the walls. The desk was clear except for a wooden box piled high with reports and memos. There was no privacy either. The walls were thin and confidence was kept only by whispering.

Rostnikov finished his sandwich and wiped crumbs onto the floor.

"And?" he asked.

Tkach chewed, hesitated.

"Nothing," he said taking another bite.

"And what is nothing?" Rostnikov persisted.

"These people are clever," the young man finally said trying not to look at Karpo. "They use words better . . . It might be a good idea to put someone else on this part of the investigation. I'm not afraid of it, but someone more . . . more able in this line might obtain more."

"You are not out there to outthink them, but to seduce them with your apparent innocence," Rostnikov said. He let out an enormous belch of satisfaction. "You let them talk, let them be clever, let them think you a fool. They will say more to prove their superiority than a clever man could get from them in combat. What do you think, Karpo?"

"We use what we have," agreed Karpo. "You must learn to use what you have."

"And I," said Rostnikov, folding his hands on his belly, "had the privilege to interview a true fool. Tell me, Karpo, did you think the K.G.B. had any fools as agents?"

Karpo's eyes turned from the sickle to the raised brown eyes of the inspector.

"It is not impossible," Karpo admitted. "There are sometimes political reasons there as there are here. It is curious, but the K.G.B. is composed of men. Men are animals. Animals are not perfect. We can only strive."

"Yes," agreed Rostnikov, "but some of us can try

harder than others, can they not?"

Karpo shrugged.

Once each month, time and duty permitting, Emil Karpo, the Tatar, the vampire, made a pilgrimage to a small café off Gorky Street. In that bar, he met Matilde, a part-time prostitute, part-time telephone operator. It was the only illegal act Emil Karpo engaged in, and he explained it to himself as the only imperfection he could not fully control in his body. A small part of him remained animal. It disturbed him, but he had learned to accept it. What he did not know was that Porfiry Rostnikov was well aware of his monthly outing and fully approved of this "weakness." If it weren't for this vulnerability, Rostnikov was sure he would have been unable to work with Karpo. He could not stand saints of any religion. Without weakness, man might no longer be an animal, but he would come close to being a robot.

There were places to go, things to do. Rostnikov would now have to make a report to Procurator Timofeyeva, and the slow-moving investigation would have to move more quickly. And then the door to the small room burst open.

Officer Yuri Grishin, a distant relative of a high official in the Moscow police, put his head in the door. It was a huge head with a face that looked as if a wall had fallen on it, but it was the family face.

"I'm sorry Inspector, but Ludmilla said I should break in and tell you. The vodka hijackers Tkach has been after. They've been cornered at a government store on Zvenigorod near the Byelorussian Railway Terminal."

Rostnikov and Tkach exchanged glances.

"Go," said Rostnikov, and Tkach rose quickly throwing on his coat.

"I would like to go too," said Karpo, placing the sickle on the desk before Rostnikov.

Tkach paused, trying to think of something to say.

"Go," sighed Rostnikov. "Go. In two hours, no more, you are to be back here and prepared to work through the night, both of you." The two junior officers left the office, and Rostnikov picked up the sickle. He looked at it, smelled it, whispered to it, cursed it, and it told him nothing. Somewhere out there was a man who could—and almost certainly would—kill again, a man who had become an animal.

Rostnikov had a sudden vision of his son Iosef and imagined him being attacked by a trio of robed Arabs carrying broken bottles and rusty sickles. To destroy the image, Rostnikov swung the sickle over his head and into the desk. Instead of sinking into the wood, it skittered along the top, making a deep scratch. At the end of the top of the desk, the sickle caught the phone and the tip of the blade broke off. There are days, thought Rostnikov, where fate denies a man even the most meaningless of dramatic gestures.

The snow had fallen all through the morning and was still falling when Karpo and Tkach got out of the *Volga* on Zvenigorod. To Tkach, the scene seemed to be played through gauze. There were vague outlines of brown-clad police with Tete guns pointed across the broad street at an old three-story building which Tkach could barely make out. There seemed to be no life on the street. If people were curious, they were not curious enough to be in range of policemen with Tete guns at the ready. It was a sleepy image of near night though the day was still with them. Tkach knew that traffic had to be rerouted on the streets around, and in the distance he could hear the angry honking of horns, a sound frowned upon and officially forbidden, as forbidden as it was to drive a dirty car in Moscow, though such things were occasionally seen.

A bundled young man with a hip holster and no machine gun hurried over to the two detectives and eagerly reported, clearly relieved to have the responsibility taken from his shoulders, which were a few years younger than Tkach's.

"Sergeant Petrov," the young man said. His face was cold and freckled. "There are three of them," he said, addressing Karpo. "They seem to be in their twenties. They are armed and have fired on us. We have waited for orders before returning fire."

"Where are they in the building?" Tkach asked.

Sergeant Petrov turned his head to the younger detective.

"We're not sure, comrade. They were in the store itself, but they may have gone anywhere in the building. They did not get away. We have all windows and the back door covered. Their car is in the rear, parked."

"What we can—" Tkach began, but was interrupted by the cracking of the window of the police *Volga* at his side. The window had been no more than a foot from his stomach and he wondered what structural weakness had caused such an accident. Something inside him answered before his mind could accommodate the information. Sasha Tkach went flat in the snow next to

Emil Karpo and Sergeant Petrov. They scrambled behind the car and waited for another shot.

"Shall we open fire?" asked the sergeant to Karpo.

Karpo raised an eyebrow and looked at Tkach.

"It's your case," said Karpo.

"Is there a way into the building with some cover?" Tkach asked.

"Yes," said the young sergeant, pointing into the gloom. "Over the roof. The store manager says there is a skylight and a short drop to the floor. It would be possible to get to the roof from the building next door. We can stretch something, and some of my men can go across."

"I'll go," Tkach said decisively, pulling out his gun to check it. He had never fired at a man before, though he had been outstanding on targets at the academy. "Karpo?"

Karpo nodded.

"We'll need one man with an automatic weapon," Tkach added.

"I'll get one and go with you," said Petrov.

"You needn't . . ." Tkach said, looking into the freckled face.

"It offends me to be shot at," the sergeant said seriously.

By working their way down the street, the trio managed to cross in five minutes. Petrov commandeered a Tete gun from one of the police, and the three made their way along the buildings on Zvenigorod. In the distance, not too far away, came a sound like a young girl laughing.

Five minutes later, the three men were on the roof

piled high with snow. Their goal was a flat room, which made it easier to extend the ladder they had brought with them from the fire truck which waited below. If the hijackers were on the other roof, the three officers could be picked off as they crossed the small chasm between the buildings. Across the street an officer on the roof signaled to them with a flashlight that the roof of the building looked clear.

Sergeant Petrov and Tkach held the ladder while Karpo began to cross.

Neither Jimmy, Coop, or Bobby knew what had happened. Jimmy was sure there had been a burglar alarm in the liquor store. Although they had heard nothing ring, it must have been connected to a local police office or something. Coop was equally sure they had been spotted. The store was supposedly closed for repairs, but someone must have come back and seen them, then run to the nearest cop. Bobby didn't know or care what had happened. He thought only that it had been a bad idea to rob the store during the day, even a dark day like this. Jimmy, who was the wildest of the trio, had seen it as a special challenge, and Coop had never allowed Jimmy to appear more brave than he, so they had ventured out.

They had one case of vodka into the car when they saw the first *Volga* with the flashing light. Coop had run for the back door, but a warning shot from outside drove him back in. They had huddled in the rear room, breathing heavily, when the voice from outside came, telling them to throw out any guns they had and come out the rear door slowly with their hands up.

Jimmy had responded by shooting out the front window and taking a shot at the *Volga* parked across the street. Return fire had been brief, and the three had scrambled up a stairway through broken glass and dripping bottles of alcohol.

Ten minutes later they had no plan.

"Maybe we should give up," Bobby said.

"They'll shoot us down when we go out the door," said Jimmy.

"Why would they do that?" Bobby said. "We haven't killed anybody."

"We shot at the police," Coop explained, his voice shaking.

"I don't think they'll kill us," Bobby said.

"They'll kill us," Jimmy said with confidence.

They could barely make out each others' faces in the daylight darkness. For minutes they sat waiting.

"Maybe we could get out over the roof," Coop suggested.

"They're up there," Jimmy countered.

Silence again.

They didn't know how much longer it had been before the new car had come and the two men without uniforms had jumped out. The three had watched the arrival from the second floor. One of the two new ones, even through the snow, looked like a skeleton.

"They called that one to kill us," said Jimmy, pointing at Karpo. "But I'll get him first."

He had fired and jumped back, unsure of whether or not he had hit the man or hit anything at all. The sound of shattering glass suggested he had missed.

"So," whispered Bobby.

"So, we wait," said Jimmy. "It's their move."

"It's just like the American movies," said Coop.

No, thought Bobby, it's not like that. It's happening.

"I'm scared," confessed Bobby to the darkness. "Let's give up. They won't kill us."

"Shut up, shut up," Jimmy shouted. Bobby thought there was a sob in Jimmy's voice, but he had never heard such a thing from Jimmy.

"It's happening," shouted Bobby. "If we don't give up, they'll kill us, kill us."

Jimmy swung out in the darkness at Bobby and missed him.

"Shut up, I said."

Jimmy stood and was ready to find Bobby and beat him, hit him, shut him up. Bobby was confusing things, making him frightened. He didn't want to die frightened.

The door through which the three young men had come burst open, and a flashlight struck them like a cold ball of snow.

"Don't move!" came a deep voice behind the light, and Jimmy fired at the voice. The room was small and the explosion of fire resounded against the eardrums of the men who were firing at vague impressions between the flashes of shots.

Then the shots stopped, and someone sobbed.

Karpo turned on the lights and kept his pistol pointed toward the place where he had first seen the three figures standing. Two thin young men stood shivering, wide-eyed with their hands in the air. One of the two had clearly wet his pants. On the ground in front of them lay a third young man with a gun in his hand. All three were wearing black leather jackets with something written on them in French or English.

"Are you all right?" Karpo asked Tkach, whose gun was leveled at the two standing young men.

"Yes. Petrov is hit."

Karpo knelt near the young sergeant.

"Stomach wound. He is alive. I'll get help."

Karpo went out the door, and Tkach moved forward across the small room, his gun leveled at the two young men, who backed away. Tkach kicked the body on the floor. He knew his first shot had hit him. It had been automatic, like hitting the targets at the range, but this one had been so much easier to hit, so much closer. He kicked the body over and looked down at the face.

"How old is he?" he asked the trembling boys. They said nothing.

"How old?" Tkach repeated.

"Fifteen, I think," said Ivan Belinkin, who would never be called Bobby again.

"No," corrected Ilya Nikolaev, who would never again be called Coop. "He was fourteen. Sasha was fourteen."

CHAPTER SIX

There were many things on the mind of Chief Inspector Porfiry Rostnikov. Though he might have denied this to others, they were, in order of priority: the safety of Iosef Rostnikov; the possibility that the killer of Granovsky and the cab driver might strike again; the chances of getting in good enough shape to participate in the weight lifting competition in June; repairing the broken toilet in his apartment.

Rostnikov brushed the hair from his eyes and fingered the scratch in his desk he had made with the sickle. He would simply lie about the broken point of the tool. There was no point in dealing with Procurator Timofeyeva on this point. Outside his office's thin pressboard walls he could hear the phone calls, the raised voices, the whispers, the movement of furniture that signaled police activity. He knew he should move, act, but unseen heavy hands kept him at his desk. To prove his activity to himself and anyone who might walk in, Rostnikov pulled out a sheet of paper and a pencil and wrote the number one.

"What is one?" he asked himself aloud. Then he wrote, "K.G.B. following Granovsky." In twenty minutes, he had a list he was rather proud of:

One—K.G.B. following Granovsky. Agent less than brilliant. On night of murder, Granovsky made several stops, according to agent Khrapenko, at home of Simon Lvov and apartment of Ilya and Marie Malenko. Both Lvov and the Malenkos were known dissidents on Tkach's primary list.

Two—Killer apparently man (woman?) in black, who killed the taxi driver about an hour after Granovsky murder, using broken vodka bottle. Both murders very bloody, very personal, unconventional weapons.

Three—Killer last seen running down Petro Street.

Conclusions: Murderer known to Granovsky? Murderer mad or very angry and so uses personal (phallic?) weapons on men? Too soon for that observation. Not politically acceptable anyway.

The part about psychology could not be discussed with others. Freud was not a popular mentor in Petrovka. That was the extent of the writing on Rostnikov's sheet except for a doodle of barbells.

Rostnikov was considering what to do next, whether to tell his wife about Iosef in Afghanistan and whether to do another doodle, when his office door opened and Karpo and Tkach stepped in. Tkach looked almost as white as Karpo.

"What happened?"

The two men sat.

"We got them," said Karpo evenly. "Three young

boys. Sasha had to kill one of them who shot a police sergeant.''

"And?'' Rostnikov went on looking at the younger officer, who seemed to be trying to gather words.

Karpo shrugged.

"The sergeant was shot in the stomach,'' he said. "Lost blood, possibly punctured kidney, broken rib, but he should survive.''

"Tkach?'' Rostnikov said with concern, putting his sheet aside.

"I don't know. He was a fourteen-year-old boy named Sasha, and I killed him.''

"He was an enemy of the state,'' Karpo said, with just a touch of irritation. "Boys of his age fought and died in the revolution and in the wars against the Japanese and the Germans. The choice was to let him kill us, and that was certainly not reasonable.''

"True,'' said Rostnikov, "but logic, political logic, the logic of the expedient present does not necessarily account for the emotion built into our bodies. We are, as you know, imperfect creatures, Emil Karpo, and some of us will never get used to killing. It is sad, but something we must face.''

"I am not immune to sarcasm, inspector,'' Karpo answered, removing his coat.

"I would hope not,'' said Rostnikov. "I was not engaged in self-indulgence but in irony, which requires our mutual cooperation and understanding.''

"Your point is taken,'' said Karpo.

"And respected?'' said Rostnikov.

"Yes.''

"An observation, Karpo. One I have wanted to make

for some time. How is it that you never blink? Is it hereditary or something you have cultivated?''

''Blinking is functionless,'' said Karpo. ''I have learned to control what appears to be a reflex but what is in fact a weakness.''

Rostnikov put up his hands and looked again at Tkach. The discussion had been indulged in to give the young officer time to recover. If he did not recover, Rostnikov was prepared to dismiss him and get someone to replace him, which would create problems, both for Tkach and the investigation.

''Shall we get back to the Granovsky murder, inspector?'' Tkach said, looking up.

Rostnikov was tempted to talk about the men he had killed, from the first when he was a soldier to the most recent, a drunk who had beaten his wife and then turned on Rostnikov with a chair when he was brought in for questioning. The first had happened so fast that it always seemed to Rostnikov as if he had imagined it. He had a captured German rifle and he had walked into a bombed-out building, a farmhouse on the road from Kiev. Other members of his squad had gone past, and he had been told by his sergeant to look inside. No one expected anything to be there, certainly not the German soldier, who had been cut off from his troops, and lunged at Rostnikov with a bayonet in his hand. Rostnikov had turned and fired at the man and plunged his own bayonet forward so quickly that it required no thought. It wasn't an act of consciousness. But there was no point in telling this to Tkach. One either accepted and learned, or one was a victim.

''Very well,'' said Rostnikov, forcing himself up

from the desk. He had sat too long and the leg had, as always, begun to stiffen. There wasn't really anyplace to pace in the small room, but he could stand and flex his joints. He could also exchange looks with Karpo, who had obviously observed the deep scratch on the desk. "You must get back to the friends or acquaintances of Granovsky, Tkach. Prepare your report on this shooting and then resume your investigation, Emil. Go to Granovsky's apartment and talk to people in the building. Maybe someone saw or heard something. Maybe someone knows of a local enemy, a nonpolitical enemy. Unlikely, but . . . who knows. Any other suggestions?"

The two men had none.

"I'm going home after I report to Procurator Timofeyeva. Call me if anything happens. Be sure to get something to eat. Now, go."

The two men left, and Rostnikov gathered up his single sheet with the doodle, placed it in a file with rough notes on his interview with the K.G.B. officer and reports from Karpo on the sickle and from Tkach on his interviews, and left to report to Comrade Timofeyeva.

At that moment, the man who had killed twice within a day sat on the floor of a small apartment, shifting a heavy iron-headed hammer from one hand to the other. Early evening darkness had come. He knew that if he moved to the window he could see only the old crumbling one-story wooden house next to his apartment building and another concrete apartment building exactly like his own no more than thirty feet away.

He had been disturbed only once during the long day. At first he had ignored the knocking at the door, but the knocking had continued with persistence and he had hidden the hammer and opened the door. The caller was a young policeman, who looked not like a policeman but a ballet dancer, asking about the murder of Aleksander Granovsky.

The game began and the killer felt no fear. He acted. He acted with subtlety, courage, conviction. He nearly wept when told of Granovsky's death and said he had been at home with his wife at the time of the murder, which was not at all true, but he was prepared to add details, little details so vivid that they would build a picture of truth.

"Terrible," he had said. "We had a quiet evening at home. We're painting the walls, as you can see. We worked. I had some newspaper gathered to back up the paint. She kept saying 'Ilyusha, we are going to run out of paint and end with three grey walls and one blue.' I told her that would be a modern look and maybe we should leave it. I'm sorry. I'm forgetting about Aleksander. Maybe I'm just trying not to face it."

"I can understand that," the young policeman had said sympathetically, but then the policeman was acting too. "It's important to find out if Aleksander Granovsky had any enemies, people who might want to do this, perhaps someone particularly volatile, emotional?"

He shook his head sadly.

"Aleksander had many enemies. Some of them were going to put him on trial this day. The enemies of Aleksander Granovsky are in the millions. He has been depicted as an enemy of the state and as you know, many fools believe in such propaganda and get carried away. You are the most likely suspect. Oh, not you personally, but the police, the K.G.B.

"You'll probably try to blame it on one of us," the killer had continued. He was leaning against the table in which he had hidden the hammer. "It will make things easier for you. I'm as good a scapegoat as you can get. Do you want to arrest me?"

"No," the young officer had said, looking quite warm and uncomfortable. "I don't want to arrest you. I simply want to know if he had any enemies. Any who might have some personal reason for wanting to kill him."

"None that I know," said the killer. "Aleksander was a good man, one who we shall miss. Another will have to be found to replace him. His voice is stilled, but there are other voices, will be other voices."

"Such as yours?" the policeman had asked, with some irritation finally showing.

The killer had shrugged. "Perhaps, but I don't think so. I think my destiny lies elsewhere. Now, if you will excuse me, I have some preparation to do before my wife comes home for dinner."

"You do not work?" the policeman had asked, with the hint of a barb in his words.

"I am a student," the killer had replied, "and as such, I quite possibly put in more hours at work than you do, and the ultimate value of my studies may have far more input to our economic future than does your pursuit of the depraved, deprived, and unfortunate. Now, if you wish to threaten me with loss of the apartment or a trip to Petrovka, please do so and then leave.''

The policeman had left with a smirk but in confusion and the killer had closed the door, retrieved the hammer and gone back to sitting on the floor.

And now he heard the footsteps in the hall. And now he heard the knock at the door. He didn't answer. And now he heard the sound of her key in the lock and the opening of the door. In the bleak light of the hall he could see her outline, the outline of his Vera. In her hand was her shopping bag filled with food she would never eat.

"Ilyusha?" she said, speaking into the darkened apartment. "Ilyusha, are you home?"

He rose from the floor as she removed her boots, still standing in the doorway. She heard him move forward and paused with one shoe off.

"You startled me," she said with a nervous smile. "Why are you in the dark?"

He waited till she took off the other boot and walked in.

"Ilyusha," she said, "what is wrong?"

"Aleksander is dead," he answered.

She dropped the shopping bag, and a sound like air escaping from a child's balloon in Gorky Park came from her dark outline. A bread skittered out, and a can of something rolled.

"I thought it would disturb you," he said. "But I have something that will disturb you even more. I killed him."

"No," she cried. "Ilyusha you . . ."

"Yes," he said, knowing that tears were coming to

his own eyes, that he would soon be unable to control his own voice. "Yes, I know. I saw the pictures. Ilyusha the-fool-no-more knows. Ilyusha who was used and laughed at."

"No," she said backing away from him. "It wasn't like that, nothing like that. You must understand."

Her coat was still on and he could sense her fear through it.

"I understand," he said, unable to hold back the tears. "Now you must understand." He brought the hammer up over his head. It was heavy up there like a barbell. He knew she could see it, could feel his weakness, and he hated both her and himself as he brought the hammer down as hard as he could as she started to whimper something softly that he never heard.

The Rostnikov toilet did not work. Well, it did work if you were willing to clean up the floor each time you flushed. So, between complaints to the regional manager who was responsible for the building, the Rostnikovs used the toilet at the end of the hall. Porfiry Rostnikov had done what he could. He had threatened the manager, a thin party member named Samsanov who wanted to talk only about his wife's illness. Threats did not work. The offer of a small bribe brought only promises and an explanation. The tenants above Rostnikov were a Bulgarian whose family was spending a year in Moscow in a technological exchange program. To fix Rostnikov's toilet meant disrupting the toilet of the Bulgarian technological expert. The Bulgarian did not know anything was wrong with the toilets. A decision had been made at a political level Rostnikov could not penetrate to keep the Bulgarian visitor from knowing that there was anything wrong with the toilet. The building manager had promised that when the Bulgarian family left in the summer, the toilet would be fixed immediately, providing of course that a higher priority political family did not move into the apartment and that a suitable bribe be involved.

Rostnikov missed his toilet. He had given up complaining as had his wife. A new idea had begun to form within him. He would go to the library, find a book about plumbing, learn how to fix the toilet and then approach the Bulgarian family directly. He did not even know if they spoke Russian, but he was sure they must in some manner. He was also of the belief that Bulgarians in general were polite people who would find it difficult to refuse his request. So, in his spare moments Porfiry Rostnikov read plumbing books.

He and his wife had eaten a quiet meal of fish soup, bread and tea with a small glass of after-dinner cognac and talked about the things they usually talked about. Rostnikov said nothing about Iosef or about the fourteen-year-old boy killed by Tkach.

Sarah was a solidly built woman of forty-five with a surprisingly unlined face considering the wear of her life. She belonged to an official national group in Russia. The Jews had to register just as did the Armenians or any other ethnic segment of the populace. Sarah was so registered. They had married after Porfiry was a policeman. If they had married before, it was almost certain that he would never have been given the job he was so good at. In fact, it was only his reputation that protected him.

He fingered the plumbing book near his plate and tore off a piece of dark bread.

"Procurator Timofeyeva does not look well," he said.

Sarah wore the familiar round Russian glasses and had a habit of looking over them when she wanted to emphasize her interest. The habit had begun when she went to work as a clerk in the Melodiya record shop on Kalinin Prospect eight years earlier. She would look over her glasses at the top of an album selected by an important customer and nod at the sagacity of the selection.

"She does too much," Rostnikov went on. "She works too hard. Loyalty and dedication have reasonable limits."

Sarah nodded in agreement.

"That young man, Tkach, shot a boy today, a robber, killed him," Rostnikov went on, looking down at his plumbing book. "You've never met him. He's a good man. Reminds me . . ."

"Of Iosef?" Sarah supplied.

Rostnikov shrugged. "In some ways. Others not."

"And you want to invite him to come over?" she said.

"Maybe, with his wife, for a drink of coffee, some time," Rostnikov went on.

"Would they accept?"

Rostnikov knew what she meant, but he felt she was oversensitive to her Jewishness. He knew, if he ever let it happen, she would open up the question of leaving Russia, of going to Israel or England or America. They had skirted the possibility many times. It was an unanswered challenge. He was not even sure what his own status was if it came to such a request. He doubted if a police official, even one as low as he, would be permitted to leave, and even to think about it publicly might end his career. There were many ways to end his career, but that might be the surest of them all. Besides, he was a Russian, a Muscovite. It wasn't just a matter of love or loyalty. It was part of him. His thoughts, past, future were within a few miles of where he now sat worrying about his son, the plumbing, a murderer, a stubborn procurator with a heart condition, a young officer fighting a sense of guilt, and a murder which made him uneasy in ways he could not quite understand.

He rose from the table, reached over with the remnants of his bread to soak up the last bit of moisture from the soup in his bowl, popped the bread in his mouth, and moved to the corner of the room.

"You shouldn't lift those things after a meal," Sarah said.

"Later I'll be too tired," he countered. Their dialogue had been almost exactly the same on this point for years, but neither could resist it. "I'm preparing for a competition."

Sarah cleared the dishes and said nothing.

"The weight lifting competition for strong old men," he said, removing his jacket and shirt and rummaging for the old sweat shirt he wore while lifting.

"Maybe you can get strong enough to lift Samsonov over your head till he promises to fix the toilet," she said, turning on the kettle on the single burner to create some hot water to clean the dishes.

Rostnikov prepared his weights. It was awkward for

him to bend with his bad knee and even more awkward to do the actual lifting. He would definitely forego, if possible, the dead lift and the clean and jerk if the competition permitted. After all, he was a war hero. Compensation should be made for that even if it couldn't get his toilet fixed.

He was into his fiftieth right arm bend with twenty-five pounds when the phone rang. He kept lifting. Almost all the calls to the apartment were police business, which was why he had the phone. But this time a finger of fear went down his back and made him shiver. It might be about Iosef.

Sarah answered. "It's for you. Karpo."

Sarah did not like Karpo. She had met him once, and he had made not the slightest attempt at being civil. Rostnikov assured her it had nothing to do with her being Jewish, that Karpo treated everyone exactly the same—badly—but Sarah did not like him.

"Rostnikov."

"Inspector, I've taken the liberty of having a car sent for you," said Karpo. There was something strange about his voice as if he felt the need to say each word precisely. "If you would meet me at the Metro entrance at Komsomol'skaya as soon as possible, I will explain. We may have the Granovsky murderer trapped. All exits are blocked."

"I'll be there quickly. You sound—" Rostnikov began.

"I have been shot," said Karpo.

Rostnikov hung up and moved across the room quickly to put on his shirt, jacket, and coat.

"I must go out," he said. "I don't know when I will be back."

"You're sweating," Sarah said. "You'll catch cold."

"I'll be in a warm car."

She nodded in resignation.

"Porfiry," she began as he opened the door.

"Yes," he said, looking back.

"As always," she said with a smile.

He returned her smile.

"There's a hockey game on the television. Why don't you watch it and report to me when I get back," he said, closing the door.

He didn't hear her say to herself, "I hate hockey."

The path that had taken Emil Karpo to the Komsomol'skaya station with a bullet in his right shoulder had begun shortly after he had left Rostnikov's office at Petrovka. He had weighed the possibility of taking a bus to Granovsky's apartment and decided he could make just as good time or better by walking the several miles. The walk in the falling snow had proved to be the easiest part of his night. When he got to the apartment building, he began systematically to question the tenants.

The knock and the announcement, "Police," got the doors open, and one look at this gaunt specter insured cooperation, but there was little to be learned from most of the people in the building. Some denied even knowing that Granovsky had lived in the building, an obvious lie. Others wanted so much to cooperate that they were prepared to describe endless streams of wild-eyed anti-revolutionary visitors. One woman, who worked in a state pharmacy, claimed that she could smell drugs on Granovsky's visitors when she passed them in the halls. An old couple named Chernov, who lived below the Granovsky apartment, complained about noise from above but could supply no leads. It soon became fairly clear to Karpo that there was little to be learned from the neighbors, but he also knew enough not to stop. Then, on the fifth floor, he had found Molka Ivanova, a woman so small as to be within a fraction of being a dwarf. She was but one of the one hundred thousand Ivanovas in Moscow, for Ivanova is a more common surname in Moscow than Smith or Jones is in New York. But she proved to be a singularly important Ivanova. Molka Ivanova was a bookstore clerk who shared her apartment with her granddaughter's family. The granddaughter knew nothing, but Molka was clearly frightened. Karpo bullied his way into the apartment. Molka's fear was not the result of a normal fear of an honest person confronting the police. She had a secret. It might mean nothing. It might mean everything. She might have a black market purchased television set or forbidden book. Karpo had no time to be discreet and no talent for it.

"The neighbors tell me you know something about the murder of Aleksander Granovsky," he said, looking down two feet at the woman with his unblinking brown eyes. Her own were fluttering rapidly and she held the top of her dress as if in fear that this ghost was going to attack her.

"It's nothing," she said, looking in the direction of her granddaughter and a teen-age boy who sat silently, pretending to pay no attention to anything but the books they held in front of them.

"Tell me the nothing," he said.

"Well . . ." she began.

"Now," he insisted with a smile that chilled the old woman.

"I did hear him . . ."

"Granovsky?"

"Yes," she said. "I heard him arguing in the hall last night walking up the stairs. I was coming back from the market. Market Number forty-seven. They had cabbage, green cabbage—"

"On the stairs," Karpo interrupted.

"They were arguing. He was threatening him."

"Someone was threatening Granovsky," Karpo supplied. "Please call him Granovsky."

"I don't know whether to call him comrade," she replied in fear.

"Do so," said Karpo.

"This man in black was drunk. He was shouting at Comrade Granovsky, saying he was disloyal, should be killed like a dog. Comrade Granovsky ignored him, and the man grabbed him. He's a big man. Comrade Granovsky spat in his face. Or the man spat in Comrade Granovsky's face. I don't remember which. It was very brief. Then Comrade Granovsky pushed the man."

The retired librarian's hands went out to demonstrate the push and stopped short of the stomach of Emil Karpo.

"Then?" urged Karpo.

"Comrade Granovsky hurried up to the sixth floor where he lives with the man behind him shouting. And that's all I heard."

And, thought Karpo, many others must have heard it too and conveniently forgotten.

"Who was this man in black? You know him." The second sentence was indeed a statement and not a question, though Karpo only sensed that it should be.

"His name is Vonovich, Mikel Vonovich. He lives down the hall in five hundred ten," Molka Ivanova said. "He is a cab driver. A big man, as tall as you but bigger across."

Karpo moved to the door and heard a voice behind him which must have been the granddaughter's.

"Don't tell him where you found out. Please."

Karpo closed the door behind him, moved down the hall, and found five hundred ten. There was no answer. Karpo had decided to get a key and examine the apartment and was turning to find the building manager when luck struck, but it is difficult to determine if it was good or bad luck for Emil Karpo.

A huge, burly figure in black with a black beard came noisily down the corridor, almost filling it, and singing a popular song twenty years old. He was somewhere in his thirty's and clearly drunk. He was about ten feet from his door before he saw Karpo.

"What?" asked Mikel Vonovich in a voice surprisingly high for his size.

"I'm from the police," Karpo announced calmly. "I would like to talk to you."

Vonovich looked to the wall on his left, then to the wall on his right and finally at the tile floor.

"What?" he bellowed.

"To talk about last night," Karpo repeated, taking a step toward the giant cabdriver.

"Last night? Last night." Something glowed in Vonovich's grey eyes and a look of cunning crossed his face. Karpo, who was prepared for either a docile change of attitude, a feigned drunkeness, or even a physical attack was unprepared for what did happen next. Vonovich reached into his pocket swaying as he bumped into a wall and came out with something in his right hand. It was a gun and it fired in Karpo's general direction. It was the second time in hours that Karpo had been shot at and once again, the shot had missed. Karpo fell against the wall, giving Vonovich enough time to turn and run down the hall into pools of light along the way—the plunge of a monster from folklore into the imaginary hell of the past. For a drunk, Vonovich moved with surprising speed.

Karpo was after him in less than a second. Not a door opened in curiosity. Not a sound was heard. Through the exit door Karpo plunged, and he could see the massive dark figure dive into a cab, his own cab surely, parked on the street. Karpo ran for it with drawn gun and shouted for Vonovich to stop. He considered shooting the cabdriver through the window but knew he would probably kill him and that he might be needed alive.

The cab ignition caught and Vonovich pulled away, skidding in the snow and almost hitting a woman and a young boy.

Karpo looked around for a car to commandeer, but there was nothing in sight but a streetcleaning truck brushing away the accumulating snow. Karpo ran to it, gun in hand.

The driver, a dark man with a grey stubble on his face, let out a gargling sound. Karpo leaped up next to the man.

"You see that cab," he said, pointing with his gun. The streetcleaner added. "Follow it. I'm a policeman."

"I can't catch a car with this," the man said logically.

"You can the way he is driving. Look."

"But—"

Karpo took the man's face in his free hand and turned it toward his own. They locked eyes for an instant, and the man pulled back.

"I'll catch him," he said dryly.

And the chase was on. The streetcleaning truck lumbered slowly forward, straight, sure, unswerving. The cab, with its drunken driver, sped for a few dozen feet, skidded, turned, stalled, started again, bounced off parked cars and hurried away.

"We will catch him," said the streetcleaner, warming to the chase. Karpo grunted.

It was late at night and traffic was light when Vonovich went backward in a skid and flew over the curb into a small park. His cab stopped just short of a pond where a few people were skating. They scattered, clutching each other. Half a block behind, Karpo leaped out of the streetcleaning truck and ran in the direction of the screams. Vonovich had abandoned his cab by the time Karpo arrived, gun in hand, to frighten the skaters. He didn't have to ask where Vonovich was. He could see him sludging forward through the park like an enormous bear.

"Stop," the policeman shouted, but the bear did not stop. It headed out of the park down a street toward the warm hole of a Metro station with Karpo behind. Karpo couldn't see Vonovich after he disappeared into the Komsomol'skaya Metro station, but he couldn't wait. He ran in just in time to see the drunken cab driver hurl himself over the stile without paying his ten kopeks and roll across the floor with a mighty "grummpf."

It was then Vonovich pulled out his gun and fired blindly in the general direction of the policeman who was pursuing him. The bullet struck Karpo in the right shoulder, knocking him back against the stairs. He could hear Vonovich hurrying, slipping down the stairs toward the platform.

"You, stop," came a voice over Karpo. "Don't reach for that gun."

It was a brown uniformed policeman leveling a pistol at Karpo who, now wounded, looked even more cadaverous than usual.

"I'm a police inspector," said Karpo.

"Yes," said the policeman, putting away his gun. "I recognize you. You're Inspector Karpo. Let me help—"

"No," shouted Karpo. "Get to the other exit. There is a big drunken man with a black beard. He is not to get away. Shoot him if you must. I'll watch this end. When is the next train?"

The policeman looked somewhat confused and tried to think.

"I don't know. Not soon. Half an hour, perhaps."

"Find out," said Karpo. "No. I'll find out. You get to the other exit. Move."

The policeman ran back up the stairs into the night, and Karpo reached for his gun. His shoulder was bleeding moderately through his coat, and his arm was numb, but his legs were fine. He went down the stairs and found a schedule on the wall. If it was right, and the Metro usually did run on time, he had time enough to call Rostnikov. He pulled himself up the stairs and made his way slowly to a public phone he had seen on the street. While watching the exit, he called Rostnikov. He looked back at the dark trail of blood spots and wondered if he should take a chance on putting his gun away and packing his wound with clean snow.

Fifteen minutes later Rostnikov had arrived. He had no trouble finding Karpo. Police cars stood at both entrances to the Metro station. Karpo sat in one of them, his arm temporarily bandaged by a policeman.

"How are you?" Rostnikov asked, sliding into the back seat next to Karpo.

"I made a mistake," said Karpo, between his teeth. "I had the chance to kill him, but I didn't take it."

"He killed Granovsky?" Rostnikov asked.

"Don't know," said Karpo. "Very possibly. But now he is down there with a gun. There are other people down there and he is drunk, perhaps mad."

"And?" asked Rostnikov trying to make his leg comfortable.

"We have about ten minutes or less till the train arrives and he gets on it."

"In that case, you better tell me what I need to know," said Rostnikov. And Karpo did just that, quickly and efficiently.

When the briefing had finished, Rostnikov emerged from the car and headed for the Metro entrance, nodding at the armed police officers who guarded it. They were all uniformed. He was about to go down the stairs when he heard the voice of Sasha Tkach behind him.

"Wait."

Rostnikov turned and watched the young man run toward him, his breath forming white clouds as he hurried forward.

"You know what we have?" Rostnikov asked.

"Enough," said Tkach and the two men went down.

The two policemen took the stairs down, talking about nonsense, the weather, life, and not looking but looking at the same time. Vonovich was easy to spot. He paced along the platform with his hands in his pockets. Certainly, he was holding his gun. A few people sat on benches talking or reading.

The first series of Moscow Metro stations built in the 1930s are comparable in design to the most decadent of castles. No two stations are alike. Komsomol'skaya, designed by two renowned artists, is one of the most baroque. It is 190 meters long and nine meters high. Its vaults are supported on seventy-two pillars. Massive mosaics depicting Russia's military past decorate the station illuminated by a series of elaborate hanging chandeliers.

Vonovich looked into the darkness down the track urging the train to come, and from the distance in the tunnel, there did come the sound of a rushing, noisy train.

Vonovich looked with suspicion at the two newcomers, who ignored him, spoke of trains and tracks, and looked at their watches impatiently. Because the short, heavy one walked with a limp, Vonovich felt somewhat reassured.

The train came hurtling out of the darkness, and both Rostnikov and Tkach knew the time for deception was over.

They walked behind a pillar, still talking, and both drew their guns.

"We do not kill him unless we must," Rostnikov whispered. Tkach nodded.

"Vonovich," Rostnikov shouted, and his voice echoed and rose above the incoming train. The boarding passengers looked around in confusion, and the heavy pacing man stopped and looked first at the train and then in the direction of the two men, who had gone behind the pillar.

"Vonovich, raise your hands and step away from the track, now!" shouted Rostnikov.

Vonovich answered with a wild shot that hit one of the massive chandeliers, sending a snow of glass to the platform. Passengers screamed and the train, which had pulled into the station, paused only for an instant with passengers inside pressing their noses to the window to see what was happening. The motorman chose not to open the doors and sped on, leaving Vonovich confused. His coat was open and swirling, and he didn't know which way to run or whether to try to hold the train back with his bare hands.

Instead, he ran for the far exit, away from the voice of the policeman, over the outstretched form of a workman who covered his head in fear and pressed his nose to the floor.

Tkach stepped out from the pillar and was prepared for pursuit, but Rostnikov held him back.

"Wait, he has nowhere to go." Then to the half-dozen people on the platform. "Stay down. Stay where you are."

Vonovich, his coat flowing open and letting out grunting sounds, hurried up the stairs and less than five seconds later came scrambling down again, obviously checked by the sight of armed police on the street.

Tkach watched the trapped man with the gun sway as he considered running down the tunnel.

"If he goes on the track," said Rostnikov, "shoot him."

But Vonovich did not. He turned his eyes back at the two policemen and began to shuffle in their direction. The shuffle turned into a run and the passengers on the platform rolled away, one woman plunging with a scream off the platform and onto the track.

Tkach and Rostnikov stepped out into the path of the rushing creature.

"If his gun comes up," said Rostnikov, "shoot. If not . . ."

But Vonovich was upon them. Tkach could feel himself shoved to the side by some animal force. He tried to keep his balance but went over a bench. Behind him he heard a loud groan and he scrambled up, gun leveled to help Rostnikov. What he saw was something he would never forget.

The massive man was struggling in the arms of Inspector Rostnikov. His legs were off the ground, churning, touching nothing. Vonovich's left arm came across in a heavy swing and Rostnikov burrowed his own head into the bigger man's coat and lifted with an expulsion of air. Tkach watched Vonovich come up in the air in Rostnikov's arms, cradled like a baby, and then Rostnikov threw the creature like a bundle of laundry into the pillar. Vonovich's gun scratched across the platform and came to rest near Tkach's leg. Vonovich himself was clearly unconscious.

As he moved forward toward the felled cab driver, Tkach could sense the passengers rising and could hear the woman who had fallen on the tracks calling for help. He could also see quite clearly that Rostnikov was smiling, a childish, satisfied smile, and looking up at a massive ceiling mosaic of an approving ancient Russian knight.

CHAPTER SEVEN

"Vonovich, have you lifted weights?" Rostnikov asked, sipping his tepid tea with loud satisfaction. Vonovich, on the other side of the desk, shifted uncomfortably.

"There is no trick to the question," Rostnikov went on. "I'm breaking the ice, making small talk. We could be here for hours and once I start with the difficult questions we might both get a headache. You, if I judge you right, will get surly. I will grow irritable. It won't be pleasant, but if we can—"

"I could tear you in half with my hands," grumbled Vonovich. "You were lucky."

The huge man grabbed the cup of tea in front of him, buried it in his brown hand and brought it angrily to his mouth spilling much of it on the way. Rostnikov sighed and took another sip of his own tea, turned from the burning eyes of his prisoner and ran his finger along the scar on his desk made by the sickle. As long as he kept this desk, which would probably be the rest of his career, that scar would be there to remind him of this case. He was determined that it would be a reminder of success and not failure, but to achieve success he would have to deal with this oaf Vonovich.

"I'm sure you could," said Rostnikov. "Shall we start the lies?"

"I have no reason to lie," growled Vonovich. "I have given you all my papers. Everything is in order."

He reached up to scratch his head and lost his hat in the process. There was little room in the office to reach for it, and the huge man almost fell out of the wooden chair.

Rostnikov shook his head giving himself—not his prisoner—sympathy. He had sent Tkach home; the boy had seen enough for one day. Karpo was in the hospital having his shoulder wound cared for. That left only Rostnikov. Now the case was his responsibility. And his pleasure.

The bears like this were a challenge, but for Rostnikov the challenge of stupidity was like that of a target for a sharpshooter. It was a matter of professional execution rather than innovation. The smart ones were often easier to break. They tried to be too clever, tell too many lies. The smart ones knew it was a deadly game, and they were confident that they could hold their own. Ah, but the stupid ones—sometimes they clung to an obviously foolish, impossible story regardless of what Rostnikov said. And though they did not know it, they were right to do it.

"What are you thinking?" demanded Vonovich, downing the last of his tea and putting his fur hat back on his head in an awkward position so that it would fall off if he moved or if gravity were simply given sufficient time.

"I was wondering how stupid you are," said Rostnikov.

"You'll see how stupid I am," Vonovich said with a cunning smile.

"Yes, I'm sure I will," agreed Rostnikov. "Why did you run from the officer in front of your apartment door?"

"I didn't know he was a policeman. He looked like a killer. A robber."

"Yes," agreed Rostnikov, reaching under the table to massage his stiff leg, "he does. So you shot at him and ran away. When you got to the street, why did you continue to run? Did you think a robber was openly pursuing you through the streets?"

"That's what I thought," agreed Vonovich, his cunning smile looking particularly stupid to Rostnikov. "I thought he was a crazy robber. There are such things. A man gets a few drinks or something and . . . there was Czekolikowski who killed everybody in the Praga Restaurant for no reason last year."

"That was five years ago," corrected Rostnikov, "and he didn't kill everybody. There are still a few Muscovites left. He shot two people, one was his brother."

"He was crazy," Vonovich insisted, crashing his fist down on the desk. Rostnikov had to catch his skittering cup, and a burly uniformed policeman who had been stationed outside the door burst in with his pistol ready.

"It's all right," Rostnikov said, holding up a calming right hand. "Comrade Vonovich is making a point." The policeman backed out, closing the door.

"I'm an honest citizen," Vonovich tried with something he must have thought was a pout.

"You are, at best a *pidzhachnik*," said Rostnikov. "You pick up a drunk or visitor and steer him into some little club where he is overcharged for vodka and a gypsy with a *balalaika* playing 'Dark Eyes.' You keep him going till he is so drunk that he can't see. Then you steal his money and his clothes and leave him in some doorway. Or you are a *fartsovschik*, a black marketeer. Where do you roam—hmm?—from the Rossiya Hotel to the Bolshoi Theater finding tourists to trade your rubles away for foreign money?"

Vonovich looked at Rostnikov warily.

"It says that about me in your files?" he asked.

Rostnikov nodded wearily, but in fact there had been very little in the file on Vonovich. There are more than ten thousand cab drivers in Moscow, and Rostnikov knew that there were not enough honest ones to fill a small cell. Vonovich was surely not one of that few.

"Why did you continue to try to escape when you saw that it was the police who were after you?" he went on.

"I was drunk," said Vonovich sadly.

"No," replied Rostnikov.

"Well, I knew it was too late. I had shot a cop. I had a gun. By then I just wanted to get away. I knew what would happen to me."

"What would happen to you?" asked Rostnikov.

"Just what is happening to me."

"Which is?"

"This."

Rostnikov wanted more tea, but that would let Vonovich know he had time to pause, to wait, to try to think. It would have to go on.

"Ivan Sharikov," said Rostnikov, looking directly into the eyes of the creature before him.

"What about him?" Vonovich answered. "Can I get more tea?"

"He's dead. No you can't, not yet."

"Water? Coffee?"

"Don't you want to know how Sharikov died?" Rostnikov tried.

Vonovich shrugged and spoke while looking at a spot on the wall above Rostnikov's head.

"He was nothing to me, another cab driver. We had words a couple of times, that's all."

"Words?"

"All you do is ask questions about everything," Vonovich burst out.

"That is my job. Yours, at the moment, is to answer them."

"I had a few arguments with Sharikov. He was a difficult, stubborn man."

"And you are as gentle as a Georgia peasant. Someone stabbed your friend in the face with a broken vodka bottle."

Vonovich shrugged again. His hat moved precariously on an angle.

"That is a chance you take when you drive a cab in Moscow at night."

"How do you know it was night?" Rostnikov jabbed.

"He drove at night. I guessed. Who knows? Who cares?"

"You killed him. That's all." Rostnikov rose as if the meeting were suddenly over, and Vonovich looked bewildered.

"That's all?" asked the giant. "You tell me I killed someone and that's all?"

"We have all the evidence we need. Where were you last night?"

"Driving my cab."

"Except," said Rostnikov sitting again, "for the time you were arguing with Aleksander Granovsky in the hall of your apartment building."

"Ha," laughed Vonovich, a single mirthless laugh. "Now you are going to say I killed him too. I was running around Moscow killing everybody as fast as I could. Bing, bing, bing."

"You tried to kill a police officer tonight," Rostnikov reminded him.

"Accident," corrected Vonovich holding up his hand. "Accident."

"The gun," Rostnikov tried.

"Left in my cab this very evening by a fare I dropped at the airport. I was going to turn it in."

"I'm taping this conversation, you know," Rostnikov said. "Do you know how stupid you sound?"

"I don't care to hear it."

"I was not offering to play it for you. Your apartment is full of stolen property. Your cab has an illegal supply of vodka. You have American money in your pocket, and you have shot a policeman. What do you think will happen to you?"

"I'll be given justice?" Vonovich asked, starting to rise. His hat fell off again.

Rostnikov sat back heavily while the giant groped for it.

"Vonovich, we know about the murder, all about the murder. We have evidence. Can't you see your bloody victim before you? Don't you want to confess and make both of our nights easier?"

Vonovich rose from the floor, hat in hand, face pale, eyes confused and still a bit drunk.

"It was an accident," he said, almost too low to be heard.

"What?" demanded Rostnikov.

"An accident. I didn't know I would . . . we fought and I just . . . I was too . . . I didn't expect him to die."

"But die he did. Where did you get the sickle?"

Vonovich looked bewildered. "Sickle?"

"You killed Granovsky with a sickle, you fool."

"Granovsky?"

"Who did you think we were talking about?" Rostnikov was up and shouting. "Did you kill someone else too?"

"I have nothing to say," said Vonovich. "I have said too much."

"You'll say more."

"No."

And Rostnikov knew that the "no" was probably all he could get for now. He had all he needed. Rostnikov turned off the tape recorder, rose, and went to the door. He opened it keeping his eyes on Vonovich, who was twisting his upper mustache.

"Take him to the cells," Rostnikov told the officer.

The policeman reached over to nudge the sitting bear, who was startled and began to rise as if to respond. Vonovich realized where he was and grew docile as he walked ahead of the policeman.

"Thank you, Comrade Inspector," Vonovich called back.

Rostnikov could think of nothing the man had to thank him for. When the policeman and prisoner were gone. Rostnikov pulled out his tape and went up to the office of Procurator Timofeyeva. She let him in almost immediately.

Young Lenin smiled down at him from the wall, and Procurator Timofeyeva sat in exactly the same position he had left her in earlier, wearing the same uniform and looking just as weary.

"And?" she said.

Rostnikov handed her the tape, which she took and placed on a machine which she pulled from a drawer. She set it up and listened intently, moving only once to adjust her glasses. When the tape ended, she snapped off the machine decisively.

"Congratulations, Comrade Rostnikov," she said with a tired smile. "You've done your job well. I'll call the Chief Procurator at once and inform him that Granovsky's murderer has been caught."

Rostnikov looked down at his hands. He was seated in the comfortable black chair before her desk and wished it were further away in a dark corner. He should certainly be quiet now, but he could not be.

"Has he?" he asked.

"Of course," said Tomofeyeva impatiently. "You have his confession. He knew both victims, quarreled with them, tried to kill a policeman.''

"I think at some time this Vonovich has quarrelled with everyone in Moscow,'' Rostnikov said, looking up. "I think this Vonovich did murder someone, but not recently and not Granovsky or the cabdriver.''

Procurator Timofeyeva looked at the pile of work on her desk and then at Rostnikov.

"Is that what you want me to tell the Procurator General, Porfiry Petrovich, that you haven't caught the murderer?''

"It is not my position to tell you what to say, Comrade Procurator,'' he answered.

"Porfiry,'' she answered in a voice Rostnikov had never heard from her before, a voice with the timber of emotion and something else. "There is so much to this. It is best that there be an end, that the murderer be this worthless enemy of the state, that the world know it was the deed of a drunken lout, a criminal. It is best.''

"As you say, comrade,'' Rostnikov agreed rising.

"Go home, rest. You have a heavy caseload. Get back to it. I'll take care of the report.''

"As you wish.''

"As I wish,'' she repeated with words far away. "There is much to be done, Porfiry, and too few of us to do it. Even after all these years the old society is still disintegrating. As Lenin told us, this disintegration is manifest in an increase of crime, hooliganism, corruption, profiteering, and outrages of every kind. To put these down requires time and an iron hand.''

"Of course,'' he said. Her hand reached out for the phone and she waited while he left and closed the door behind him.

Rostnikov picked up his coat in his office and went home. He could not justify a police car now so he took the bus and walked telling himself it was over but realizing that he could not accept this. Oh, he could accept it with his body and go on with his caseload. It would not be the first case that ended without a solution or with one that Rostnikov thought was wrong. No, this one would continue to bother him because if Vonovich were not the killer then the killer was still out there in one of the buildings he was passing or a hotel or walking the streets.

Rostnikov had difficulty accepting the priorities of his society. He recognized them, understood them, sympathized with them, but it was difficult. He had perhaps read too little Lenin and too much Dostoyevsky, or maybe too many of the American police stories that he had bought from Chernov the bookseller, the stories in which Ed McBain's 87 Precinct Police always got their man or woman. If he ever got to America, Rostnikov wanted to meet Ed McBain, or at least visit the city of Isola.

Sarah had a pot of soup and a half loaf of black bread ready for him when he got home.

"It's finished?" she asked.

He shrugged and looked over in the corner toward his beloved weights, but he was too tired. He should rise above his weariness and do some lifting, show his resolve.

"The hell with it," he said instead with a huge glob of bread in his mouth.

"What?" asked Sarah.

"Nothing," he said and reached for his plumbing book.

Anna Timofeyeva had a cat. It was one of the few things in her life about which she felt guilty, for she spent very little time with the animal. Home, except for the cat, was where Anna went because it was improper to sleep in her office.

"I hear, Bakunin," she told the ancient grey fluff that waddled toward her as she took off her coat, "that in America they have special food for cats, special food. You go to the store and stand in line for cat food."

In spite of her position, Anna Timofeyeva lived in a small one-room apartment in an old one-floor concrete building that had originally been built as a barracks for an artillery unit. When the site was abandoned after ground-to-air missiles were developed, the barracks along the Moscow River were converted into small apartments with a communal kitchen which had once served as the kitchen for the artillery unit stationed within its walls. Anna Timofeyeva felt comfortable in the small room. It required little cleaning, was conveniently located and quite practical.

It was somewhere around three in the morning, she knew, but she had no interest in checking the time. The important time was when she got up, not when she went to sleep. She had named the cat Bakunin, for the infamous anarchist who had opposed Marx, because she liked to think the cat was an adventurous troublemaker who had to be forgiven. Bakunin purred loudly and rubbed against her as she pulled a can of herring from her pocket. Bakunin was, in fact, a remarkably docile creature who, having been denied the opportunity to roam, became like a beast in a zoo, dependent on the one who feeds him and in a general state of physical torpor with occasional moments of undefined resentment.

"Patience, Baku, patience," she said, finding her can opener and working on the herring. "We must learn patience." And, she thought, above all we must learn to compromise.

Although she was hungry, Anna Timofeyeva knew that sleep was more important to her. She would not go down to the kitchen to cook something or even make some tea. Such an act would disturb the other tenants. Not that they would complain. They all deferred to Comrade Timofeyeva, who was a legend in the building, a legend seldom viewed but often discussed. That one of her high rank should live among a group of the relatively poor was most puzzling. The tenants vacillated between extreme suspicion and fear and pride, believing that somehow her presence provided those under the roof with a special protection.

She had lived in the building for more than twenty years, but Anna Timofeyeva was barely aware of the other tenants. She knew that at least one of the other six was a family with a small baby that occasionally awoke crying in the middle of the night.

After rubbing her eyes, Anna Timofeyeva allowed herself to move to her bed where she slowly pried at the can of herring with an old metal opener. The cat purred loudly, and Anna moved surely with thick, strong fingers.

"Allow me a taste," she said dipping her fingers past the jagged edges of metal. "It passes inspection." She put the can on the tile floor and leaned over to pet the cat as it ate.

"Bakunin," she whispered. "Lenin said that to reject compromises 'on principle,' to reject the permissibility of compromises in general, no matter of what kind, is childishness, difficult even to consider seriously. Sometimes I think Rostnikov fails to understand the nature and need for compromise."

Bakunin was working on a particularly unresponsive piece of fish which dangled from the corner of his mouth.

Anna Timofeyeva removed her uniform carefully, brushed it, and hung it on the high hook where Bakunin could not rub against it. There was no mirror in the room. Anna Timofeyeva was only interested in her image insofar as it displayed conviction and authority and that she could see in the window in the morning.

She changed her warm, practical woolen underwear and moved to the small basin in the corner to brush her teeth with salt and a calloused finger. Something tugged at her chest like a marionette master pulling all the strings at once, and then it passed. She breathed deeply, rinsed her mouth and retrieved one of the small pills that had been given her by the doctor at the Institute Sklefasofskala. The tightness slowly passed as the pill began to work.

"Bakunin," she said softly. "I must straighten the room." She moved slowly, putting what little there was to put in order in the right place and then she removed the note from her dresser drawer. It was a simple note that she had prepared three years before. It stated that if she were to be found dead, instructions for the continuance of her cases were in the top drawer of the desk in her office. Her instruction book was brought up-to-date each day before she came home to sleep. Her note asked that Bakunin be given to Rostnikov in the event of her death, but she had made no provisions for the eventuality of going to a hospital.

Her principal fear, as she turned off the light and got into bed under the woolen blanket, was not that she would die at night, but that she would simply suffer a heart attack and live. Her nightmare was that she would lie helpless while someone in the building heard her gasps and dialed 002 for "fast help." She could imagine the big white ambulance with its red cross and its soft siren pulling up in front of the building and the attendants coming in to lift her from the bed and take her out.

The cat finished chewing down a bit of fish, and she could hear it in the darkness lapping at the bowl of water on the floor. Then the animal leaped softly to the bed and sought the warmth of Anna's solid body.

"The worst thing," she whispered to the cat as she stroked it, "is not to be useful."

Someone padded down the hall outside her door, moving toward the communal toilet, and somewhere else in the distance, a car hummed down the street.

"I'll not sleep this night," she told her cat, resisting the urge to roll on her side for greater comfort. The doctor had told her to sleep on her back. "I'll not sleep."

She slept.

CHAPTER EIGHT

Sasha Tkach was disturbed when he woke up. He had slept soundly and dreamed not at all of the boy he had killed the previous day. He felt guilty about his lack of guilt. He should have tossed and turned and wept and worried, but he had not. He had slept comfortably with one arm around Maya. In fact, just before he had fallen asleep, he had a strong urge to make love to her, and he felt she would have responded, but the guilt had been too much, or at least the feeling that he should feel guilty.

"Do you understand?" he had whispered to Maya, so they would not wake his mother in the next room.

"You don't feel guilty," she said, touching his face.

"I should, shouldn't I?"

"I don't know. I don't think so."

"I'm growing insensitive," he whispered.

"You are being honest. It is too bad the boy is dead, but you didn't know him. He meant nothing to you. You had invested nothing in him and you killed him while doing your work. You are probably a bit ashamed of being proud.''

''Perhaps,'' he mused. ''It is difficult to be a policeman.''

''It is difficult to be anyone in Moscow,'' Maya said, sitting up.

And then it struck Tkach. He pushed his yellow hair from his face and remembered. Sasha Tkach was unaware that the case was over, that Vonovich the cab driver had confessed, that he was to go back to his regular caseload. Tkach was not aware that he was about to disrupt a politically tranquil situation. He was simply being a policeman. He leaped up and went to his pants searching for his notebook.

''What are you doing?'' Maya whispered from the stove where she was turning on the kettle.

''Looking for . . . aha, here,'' he said.

''Sasha, what's wrong?'' came his mother's voice from the next room.

''Nothing mother. Go back to sleep.'' He looked at his notes again and there it was. He should have put it together. It might be nothing, but he should have seen it. He was sure Rostnikov and Karpo would have seen it, but he had not tied it together.

''I have to go quickly,'' he said to Maya, slipping into his pants.

''All right,'' she said. ''Take the sandwiches, and don't eat them too early.''

He took them and grabbed for his coat on the wall. ''And don't worry.''

''Worry?'' he asked.

''About the boy,'' she said.

And then he felt a terrible guilt.

In twenty minutes he stood before the apartment building he was seeking. He had been there the day before, had interviewed a young man, a confident young man, one of four people he had talked to, friends or acquaintances of Aleksander Granovsky. This one had really been no different. The difference was that he lived on Petro Street. Petro Street was where the cab driver had been killed. True it was at least a mile from here, but he remembered the two witnesses who had reported that the killer looked young and had headed down Petro Street. He had accepted the young man's alibi too easily. He had to check with the man's wife.

When he had looked up the names of the Granovsky friends, the Petro address had simply been one of them. In fact, it was probably nothing, a coincidence, but he should have noticed. Tkach bounded up the stairs and down the dark hall.

"Ilyusha Malenko," he called after he knocked. There was no answer. He knocked again and called again.

He tried the door but it was locked. Five minutes later he found the building superintendent, who was unimpressed by the police officer. She was a stout woman in her thirties with stringy red hair and a permanent scowl.

"The Malenkos are quiet people," she said.

"I don't care about that," Tkach answered impatiently.

"I know they have some friends whom they should not have, but they are young. They will learn. We have to support our comrades. Besides," she said leaning toward Tkach, "young Malenko's father is a man with influence."

"I want the door open now," demanded Tkach.

127

"And if I say 'no?' " she said with hands on ample hips.

"I'll have you arrested," he said slowly. "You are obstructing an investigation of murder. In fact, I think you have gone too far already."

"Wait," said the woman searching in her apron pocket. "I'm just being careful. I have a responsible job."

Tkach took a particular delight in frightening the woman. He had never had any success in influencing his own building superintendent, who did not look radically different from the one before him.

She wobbled down the corridor ahead of him and grunted up the stairs. He followed, wondering what he would find in his search. Maybe something incriminating, some evidence of a sickle, something. In fact, though he was excited by what he was doing, he also hoped that he would find nothing, expected that he would find nothing and that Malenko's wife would say he had been quietly at home when the murders were committed.

"All right, it's open," said the red-haired woman stepping in ahead of him. "Now what you think you will find is . . ."

Tkach had been right behind her when she suddenly backed up. Her wide rear hit him in mid-stomach, and they both tumbled to the hall floor. Tkach's breath was gone, and he struggled to push the heavy burden from him so he could try to resume living.

His first thought when he saw her face was that she was having a heart attack. The woman's eyes were wide with fright, and she was gurgling. Mouth-to-mouth resuscitation would be essential, but the idea repulsed him and he considered seriously letting her die. Instead of dying, she pointed to the room. Tkach forced himself up, pulled out his gun, and moved into the room doubled over, though he was now getting air. What he saw straightened him up and filled him with nausea.

The figure swayed above him in the room, strung up by a man's tie to a rod which was used to separate the room into two halves. The figure was all red and that of a woman. He could tell from the dress. He certainly could not tell from the face. There was no face, just a pulpy mass of blood.

There was no one else in the room. Had there been he could easily have smashed Tkach's brains and walked out even though the detective was armed, because the detective was also hypnotized by the image before him. He didn't want to think of his first impression, but it came up at him as his eyes held fast on the gently swaying body. His first impression was that he was looking up at the corpse of his own Maya. He knew he was going to be sick, but he didn't want it to happen in here where he would have to explain it. He went out the door, tripped over the superintendent, who screamed, and raced for the cold outside.

Emil Karpo did not spend the night in the hospital, though he was advised to do so. His wound was not bad, though he had to wear a bandage and sling. The pain was greater than he would have expected, but he did not fear pain. The hospital was too protective and protected. Emil Karpo wanted to be somewhere where he could count on the help of Emil Karpo, and that somewhere was in his room. He had slept for six hours and then arose in the morning with an arm so sore that any movement was agony. His first act, after forcing his pants on with one hand, was to call Petrovka, where he found out that Vonovich was being held for the murder of Aleksander Granovsky.

He was told by Rostnikov to take the rest of the week off. His protest was overridden, and a compromise was reached. Karpo would take the day off to rest. He hung up and went back to his room to rest, but he knew he would not rest. There was nothing wrong with his feet or his head. He could work, must work. Every day that went by without catching a criminal meant another day for another crime. In spite of social change and the clear needs of the state, people continued to commit crimes against each other, and it remained the responsibility of Emil Karpo to do his best to keep the criminals in check.

So Karpo dressed. It was painful and took almost half an hour, but he did it and did it alone. Since he knew no one in his apartment building with any intimacy or cordiality, that was the way he would have to have done it anyway.

He was on his way out of the building when the phone rang in his room, but he did not hear it. It was, in fact, Rostnikov calling to tell him of a call he had just received from Sasha Tkach on Petro Street.

Karpo decided his task for the day would be a relatively easy one. He had a few suspects to check in the case of the person who was impersonating a police officer and preying on the African students. It was a short list of people who had been arrested for crimes committed while in some kind of disguise or uniform. The first name on the list was that of Vasily Kusnitsov also known as Chaplin because he liked to think that he looked like Charlie Chaplin. Kusnitsov was not home.

The next name on his list was that of Rudolf Kroft, a former circus performer who had come on bad times after injuring his leg in a fall. He had twice been arrested for posing as a bus driver and a census taker. The house on Meduedkoya Street was not difficult to find, but it was an incredible house. Karpo thought that a good breath of air or another touch of snow would be enough to send the old wooden building tumbling. He walked gently up the steps of the three-story building and opened the door. The little alcove was cold as the outside. Karpo resisted the desire to rub his sore arm and examined the names on the wall. Kroft was on the top floor. He made his way up the creaking stairs finding that it grew no warmer as he rose. The room he sought was right at the top and he knocked.

"Kroft," he said. "I want to talk to you. Police."

"I've done nothing," insisted the frightened voice inside.

"We'll talk about it when you open the door."

Karpo heard a shuffling sound on the other side of the wooden door and something that sounded like the opening of a window. He took a step back in the narrow hall, lifted his foot, and kicked at the door. It gave as if it had been sucked in by a vacuum, and Karpo skidded across the floor of a room even smaller than his own. His eyes saw two things immediately: a police uniform laid neatly on the small bed and a frightened little man in his underwear standing next to it. The frightened little man, in turn, saw the angel of death that had broken down his door, and he turned and leaped out of the window.

Karpo hurried across the room and to the window to look down for the body, but there was no body. There was no impression in the snow three floors below. Then the answer came. Snow fell from above onto Karpo's head, and he looked up. The overhang of the roof was inches over his head, and he could hear the scuttling of feet on the roof.

With just one hand, he knew he could not follow Kroft, but he was equally determined that he would not let the criminal get away. He went back in the room and out the door, looking up and around. He began kicking down doors.

The first room was unoccupied at the moment except for a huge photograph of a naked woman. The photograph looked very old. In the next room whose door he kicked down, an old woman was talking to a small child. The woman screamed without sound, and the child—Karpo could not tell if it was a boy or girl— looked at him blankly. He paid no attention to them but leaped to the ladder nailed to the wall. He banged his sore arm against the wall and made his way awkwardly up, having to let go at each step and grab for the wooden rung above. He took splinters in his hand, but fortunately there was a very low ceiling and the rungs were few. He forced open the trap door covered with snow by pushing his head against it. It gave slowly, struggling with him for supremacy, but Karpo was a stubborn man with a strong head. He worked his way up on the sloped roof and looked around for Kroft.

"Kroft," he called. "Give up. There is no place to escape."

"I could have killed you," a voice came from behind Karpo. As he turned to face it, his feet gave way in the snow, and Karpo began to fall toward the edge of the roof. He went down on his arm and immediately felt an agonizing pain and heard something crack. Suddenly a sure hand grabbed his sleeve and pulled him.

"Are you all right?" said Kroft, looking into his face.

"Yes," said Karpo struggling to get up. "You are under arrest."

"I know," said Kroft, who stood shivering in his underwear, "but all the same, I could have simply pushed you off the roof. You shouldn't be climbing around with an arm like that."

"That is my concern," said Karpo, unable to resist the help of the man in underwear. "Now go ahead of me down the ladder, and don't try anything or I'll have to shoot."

Kroft shivered and shrugged his shoulders.

"There's a little boy in that room," he said. "You think I'd want you to shoot? For a policeman you don't think much about the people you're supposed to be helping."

"I don't need lectures from a criminal," said Karpo. "Now down."

And Kroft went slowly down the ladder with Karpo struggling behind him, but the struggle was in vain. The policeman fell to the floor dropping his gun beneath him. He tried to roll over and extract the weapon from the weight of his own body but found the pain in his arm nearly unbearable. When he finally did retrieve the weapon and looked around, he saw Kroft on a small bed in the corner with a blanket wrapped around his legs. The old woman and the boy looked at Karpo expressionlessly, as if they were now quite accustomed to people in their underwear and wounded men with waving pistols going through their little room.

Karpo was drenched in sweat and unable to come to a sitting position.

"Don't move," he warned Kroft.

Kroft touched his nose with his hand, clutching the blanket to him tightly for warmth, not modesty.

"If I wanted to move, I could have run while you were squirming around down there like a turtle on its back. I'll help you up."

He got up and started to hobble toward Karpo who waved him back.

"Don't move, I said."

"If I don't help you, you will sit there till Moscow turns capitalist, and I will wither away," Kroft said reasonably.

"Why didn't you run?" Karpo demanded, trying to find a reasonable way to at least come to a sitting position.

"Where would I run? I could grab my pants and go out the door. Where would I sleep? Who do I know well enough to hide me? The circus people would turn me in. My relatives are two thousand miles away. Why should I make you even angrier than you are with me? This way I go to trial. I say I'm sorry. I repent. I tell the judge I don't know what got into me. Maybe I'll even blame decadent French novels and magazines for my folly.

Confession is a marvelous tool. Maybe my sentence will be light.''

"You are a parasite," hissed Karpo bewildered by his predicament.

"Perhaps," agreed Kroft. "But would I be less of a parasite if I didn't work at all? No one wants to hire a sixty-year-old arielist with a bad leg and a prison record.''

"You are sixty-two," Karpo corrected.

"Look at him," Kroft appealed to the old woman and the boy. "He lies there in helpless agony and he can't help arguing with me about a few years. What is your name?''

"Deputy Inspector Karpo, but that is not meaningful at present. You can help me up, but do so carefully.''

"Thank you, Mister Detective Inspector Karpo," Kroft said with sarcasm and a deep bow. "It will be an honor to help such a fine fellow as you. Perhaps you will bear in mind my consideration when you testify at my trial, if I am to have one.''

With Kroft's help and the watchful eyes of the old woman and boy, Karpo stood on wobbly legs. He almost fell, but Kroft helped him.

"Are they so short-handed that they send wounded police out to catch criminals?" Kroft asked as he helped Karpo to the door. "Or am I so insignificant a criminal that I merit only the lame for my pursuer?''

"Parasite," repeated Karpo.

"I didn't rob a single Russian," Kroft insisted helping Karpo down the hall to his room. "Not a single Russian, only Africans and Indians. If I had not done this, I would have indeed been a parasite on the state, which would have fed and clothed me. Look how I live. You think I get rich being a criminal? What about the real criminals who take government contracts to make one thing and make something else more profitable instead?''

"Dress," said Karpo, leaning against the door as Kroft reached for his pants.

"Not the uniform," Karpo had to bark. Kroft shrugged and laid it aside, saying, "It's the only decent clothing I own."

In a few minutes, Kroft was dressed, and Karpo was ready to pass out from the pain.

"Public enemy number two, as the Americans say, is ready," sighed Kroft.

His coat was indeed badly frayed and his hat a worn cloth affair.

"Perhaps it is better I look like this," sighed Kroft. "You know, play for sympathy, though I far prefer dignity even at the price that must be paid for it." He looked at Karpo for an answer but got none, so Kroft went on. "I know. I know. Muscovites are all philosophers. Let's go, if you can make it."

It took them almost four minutes to get down the three flights of stairs and another ten minutes to find a taxi. The driver didn't want to stop, but Kroft had leaped out in front of him.

"This is a policeman," he shouted at the red-faced driver. "A policeman. We are both policemen. Take us to Petrovka."

Along the way, Karpo passed out twice, regaining consciousness in a kind of dim twilight. He had no recollection of ever reaching Petrovka or being helped in and up the stairs by his prisoner.

"It is a brochure, a pamphlet advertising an English aftershave lotion, a kind of perfume for men," Rostnikov told Inspector Vostok. Vostok could not read English and had brought the odd piece of paper into Rostnikov's office. It was well known that Rostnikov read English well though it was not generally known that this familiarity came primarily from reading black market American mystery novels.

"A perfume for men," the burly Vostok repeated incredulously. "For men to wear, like the aristocrats before the Revolution?"

"Yes," agreed Rostnikov.

"Like women in France?" Inspector Vostok continued.

"Something like that," agreed Rostnikov. "Where did you get it?"

"In the room of one of those three boys, the ones who were caught robbing the liquor store," Vostok said, staring at the paper in his ruddy hands.

"The dead boy's room?" asked Rostnikov.

Vostok shrugged. "I don't know." And then he was gone.

This was the point at which Tkach had reached Rostnikov by phone, after which Rostnikov called and missed Karpo. He immediately ordered a car and headed for Petro Street. The driver was the same one who had taken him to Granovsky's two nights earlier. He said nothing, which suited Rostnikov.

Tkach was standing in the door of the Malenko apartment, transfixed by the bloody figure of the dead woman. It was still morning, and the bright light of day made every detail of the scene clear and repulsively beautiful.

"Three in two days," Rostnikov said easing past the younger man. "Did you call the evidence people?"

"Yes, immediately after I called you," said Tkach.

"Good, have you looked around?"

"Yes," said Tkach. "The murder weapon appears to be a hammer found on the floor. No good fingerprints on it. I can find no picture of Ilyusha Malenko but I will find one and get it out to the uniformed . . ."

Rostnikov looked up at the corpse and wondered at the fury that had caused such an assault.

"You think the husband did this, then?" he said.

"Yes, of course. He killed Granovsky, the cab driver, and his wife."

"Hmmm," said Rostnikov. "You don't think the poor man could simply be wandering around Moscow or at school or visiting, unaware that someone has done this?"

"No," said Tkach. "It is so unlikely as to not be reasonable. He lives on Petro Street, and his wife and friend are both killed within a day's time."

"Maybe he is scheduled to be the next victim," Rostnikov tried.

Tkach was confused but convinced of his observation.

"No, I talked to him yesterday. He was strange. I can see that now. When we find him, I'm sure we will find the murderer."

"His motive," said Rostnikov opening a dresser drawer. "Why?"

"He is clearly mad," Tkach almost laughed.

"Yes," nodded Rostnikov, "but even a madman has reasons, even mad reasons. He didn't kill you yesterday. There are certainly others he has met in the last two days whom he has not felt the need to murder with some tool at hand."

"I don't know," said Tkach. "We can find that out when we find him."

"Yes," said Rostnikov, "but if we know why he did these things, the possibility would exist to prevent him from doing even more."

"I see," said Tkach.

"Then, while we are trying to find Ilya Malenko, it might be a good idea to see some more of his and Granovsky's friends to try to puzzle this out. Take your list and go."

Tkach went and Rostnikov stood alone. He had avoided staring at the corpse with Tkach present. Now he felt himself compelled to do so, not for professional reasons, but for reasons he could not fully understand. He felt the need to reach up and take her down. He could do it easily. Her weight was nothing. There was so little of her, but it was a weight he could not lift. She was an accusing weight.

An hour later he was back in Procurator Timofeyeva's office, in the same black chair, the same cold room. He watched the square of a woman eat a sandwich and drink some tea at her desk. She looked as if she had not slept. She had offered him tea, but he had refused. His task would not be easy.

"So," he said. "There is reason to believe that Ilya Malenko killed Granovsky."

"Not necessarily," she said, holding up a finger to which a large bread crumb adhered. "He could have killed his wife and Vonovich have killed the others."

"Possible," said Rostnikov. "Very coincidental. We don't have that many murders in Moscow. Even if Malenko didn't kill his wife it is certain that Vonovich, who was with us, did not do it. There is a connection."

Procurator Timofeyeva removed her glasses and massaged the bridge of her nose with her thumb and forefinger never putting down the sandwich of stale bread, and savoring every bit of gastronomical discomfort.

"Not necessarily," she said.

"As you say, Comrade Procurator," Rostnikov agreed. "However, I may assume that I can pursue the murderer of Marie Malenko?"

Procurator Timofeyeva rose, her face a sudden crimson, and threw her sandwich on the desk. The sandwich crumbled, confirming Rostnikov's belief that it was stale.

"Rostnikov, it is not that simple. There are political ramifications that go beyond—"

"Beyond catching the right murderer?" Rostnikov continued.

"Perhaps even that," she shouted, retrieving the parts of her scattered cheese sandwich. "Perhaps even that. The state and its needs go beyond the justice of one particular murder. We are not naïve Swedes or Americans who place such simple concepts up as truths which will rule the world and make men just, true, and honorable. Choices must be made. There are few absolutes. There are just situations."

"Am I to ignore this last murder, then?" he asked as innocently as he could.

Procurator Timofeyeva sipped some tea and looked at him.

"No," she said. "Go ahead, but report what you find to me. At the moment the Granovsky murder is solved, the murderer has been caught. If we find that this Malenko killed his wife, it is another matter, another crime. You are not to connect the murders in any way without first discussing the situation with me. You understand?"

"Yes, Comrade Procurator."

"Then you may get back to work," she said, looking up to Lenin for inspiration. "And Porfiry, heed my words. Be careful."

He closed the door behind him and went back to his office. The barking of the police dogs coming off of another shift came to him from afar. Back in his office, he found his two guest seats occupied. In one slumbered Emil Karpo, his bandaged arm dirty. In the other sat a ragged, docile, little man.

"I think he needs a doctor," said the man as soon as Rostnikov entered.

Rostnikov went to his phone and barked an order into it and then hung up.

"He insisted on coming here," the man said looking protectively at Karpo.

"And you?" asked Rostnikov. "Who are you?"

"An actor," said Kroft.

"Then thank you actor and you may go after you fill

out a report on what happened,'' said Rostnikov, who moved to examine Karpo.

''I'm an actor first and a criminal second,'' the man said. ''He was arresting me when he got hurt. I greatly respect the police, but don't you think you should be more careful of those you send out on such assignments?''

Karpo seemed to be more in a coma than asleep, and Rostnikov went back to his chair. He and Kroft looked at each other.

''You remind me a little of Ibiensky, the strong man in the circus,'' Kroft observed.

Rostnikov woke from his thoughts and examined the man, who suddenly seemed much wiser and more perceptive.

''I lift weights,'' Rostnikov answered.

''I could tell,'' said Kroft with satisfaction, rubbing the grey stubble on his chin. ''I was with the circus for almost thirty-five years. I learned all of Ibiensky's tricks.''

Rostnikov's eyes lit with interest, and he leaned forward.

''You did?'' he asked.

CHAPTER NINE

"Where is the other driver?" Rostnikov asked settling into the rear of the police *Volga*. The temperature had crept up to nineteen or twenty degrees fahrenheit, with no snow falling. He could have taken a train, but he would have spent a good part of his day in transportation, and Procurator Timofeyeva had urged him to conclude his investigation swiftly.

"He is ill," said the new driver pulling into the street and looking over his shoulder.

This one, thought Rostnikov, has an intelligent face. Let us hope the face does not hide a talkative personality.

"What is his malady?" Rostnikov asked, going over the notes in his notebook.

"American flu," said the driver.

"I understand they call it Russian flu in the United States," Rostnikov replied.

"I know little of American prejudices," said the driver. Rostnikov examined him further. He was young, with close-cut brown hair under his fur cap. He looked like an athlete in some track or field sport.

"I know of them through occasional reading of American novels," said Rostnikov, looking out of the window into the glaring sun.

"I cannot read American novels," said the driver. "I can't keep the names straight. Americans have so many strange names, so many variations and diminuitives. I can never keep it straight. For example, an American can have the names John, Jack, Jonathan, Johnny—and all be the same person."

"And your name?" asked Rostnikov, willing to carry on the conversation because he did not look forward to the interview he was about to undertake.

"Dolguruki. Michael Veselivitch Dolguruki."

That ended the conversation. Rostnikov could think of nothing further to say. Had he been sitting in the front seat, he might have found it easier. In fact, he had observed that other inspectors and even government officials and the wealthy and elite tended to sit in the front seats with their drivers as acts of social equality, as if everyone did not know that they were far from equal. Rostnikov preferred the space of the back seat and the solitude.

Rostnikov was being silently jostled as the car moved expertly through the wide black asphalt streets jammed with late morning trucks spitting exhaust and with swarms of cars—*Volgas, Muskvitches, Laplas,* and tiny *Zaporojetzes*—jockeying for the curb as if in a race or game. They drove through old Moscow, just outside the walls of the Kremlin with houses one-hundred-fifty years old side by side with new concrete blocks with few windows that looked like untreated marble ready for a sculptor to release the imprisoned figure or figures frozen within it. They passed the ministries and went through the small side streets with wooden houses that looked ready to fall and had looked that way a dozen or more years before the Revolution.

The driver found Leningrad Prospect and headed out to Volokolamsk Highway. The last circle one encounters in moving away from Moscow is that of the *dacha* suburbs where many wealthy Muscovites have their summer villas. This circle is, ironically, also shared by the poorest of the Muscovites, those who cannot afford to live closer to the city where they work and are forced to exist in shacks of one room which tourists are steered away from. So only those who can afford to travel easily to the inner city and those who are least able to do so, share this ring. It was here, on Moscow Ring Road, that they were heading now.

Rostnikov did not enjoy this task. He had called at a suitable hour in the morning, a time that seemed not too early to wake up anyone at the house and not too late to miss the person he was trying to reach. He had gotten someone, a woman, and explained his mission and was given an appointment for the next hour. It gave him little time to prepare, but he preferred the discomfort of the encounter and the lack of preparation to the alternative, the continued freedom of a brutal killer who was most likely Ilya Malenko.

He had taken upon himself the responsibility for tapping the phones of Malenko's various known acquaintances in the hope that the man would try to contact one of them. In addition, Tkach would go to each of the dozen or so people on the list and inform them of the gravity of the situation if Malenko should try to reach them other than by phone. There was some hope that at least some of them would cooperate, not for political reasons or fear, but because Malenko had murdered Granovsky and Marie Malenko. Of course, he might contact no one, but that was unlikely. He could get no work without identifying himself. He would have nowhere to stay without contacting a friend or relative.

The most likely person to contact was obvious and that, indeed, was the person with whom Rostnikov had made the appointment. Although he had been in this area of *dachas* in which they found themselves, Rostnikov was not really familiar with them. It was an alien world normally denied him and other policemen. When crime occurred by or to the members of this cultural elite, it was invariably handled by the K.G.B. or the militia.

The driver found the house with little difficulty and pulled into the small driveway in front. It was a two-story home, wood and brick, freshly painted from the summer. Rostnikov got out and the driver began to follow.

"You remain here," said Rostnikov, motioning the man back without looking at him.

"As you wish, Comrade Inspector," was the reply, and Rostnikov heard the car door close behind him. He walked to the front door, anxious, apprehensive and a bit angry, angry that he should feel this way. This was the home of a rich man, not one who was rewarded for his achievements in the arts or sciences or government or even athletics, but a man who everyone knew had grown rich by black market connections, by alterations of government manufacturing contracts, by bribes— yes even massive bribes to the police. It was known and he was tolerated. No, he was not just tolerated, he was supported, one of the hidden capitalists who helped the economy and were purposefully overlooked.

Rostnikov knocked. The door was solid and painted white. Inside he could hear footsteps on a hard floor and the door opened. A woman, a very beautiful woman somewhere in her thirties, opened the door and smiled at him with teeth Rostnikov thought impossible to maintain in Moscow. Her eyes were so blue that they seemed to be painted and her straight yellow hair was swept back like a Frenchwoman's.

"You are Inspector Rossof?" she said.

"Rostnikov," he corrected.

"Yes," she said, stepping back to let him in. "Sergei was on his way out of the door when you called this morning. I just caught him."

They stood in a small hallway with dark wooden floors.

"I did not mean to . . ." Rostnikov began.

"That's all right," she stopped him with a smile. "Come, he is in the parlor."

Rostnikov followed her a few steps. She stopped and turned around.

"It is Ilyusha, isn't it?" she said softly, her smile suddenly vanishing.

"Your . . ." Rostnikov began not sure of the relationship of this woman and the man he was pursuing.

"My stepson," she said coming to his aid. "I don't

really know him. I actually only met him once and we didn't get on.''

"I see,'' said Rostnikov sagely, though he didn't see why she was telling him this.

Her smile returned. "I don't even know what he has been doing, what his interests are,'' she said, and Rostnikov understood. This woman wanted to make it clear that she was no part of Malenko's political position or anything else he might be involved in.

"I see,'' he said, and this time he did.

"I was a clerk in my husband's factory when Ilyusha—''

Her statement was interrupted by the opening of the door before which she stood. She stepped back as if the sound had brought with it a terrible blast of heat.

"Elizabeth,'' said the man who now stood before them, "I must get to town for that meeting with the under-minister. I'd appreciate seeing the inspector immediately.''

"I'm sorry,'' Elizabeth Malenko said, unable to keep from looking around the hallway at all she might lose by offending the important man.

"It's all right,'' the man said. "Perhaps the inspector would like some tea or coffee.''

"Coffee would be fine,'' said Rostnikov, wondering if a cup of coffee constituted the first step in a bribe.

The woman disappeared through another door, and the man backed up to let Rostnikov enter the room.

In the doorway, Sergei Malenko had simply seemed a middle-size, middle-shaped man, but inside the surprisingly large room, he reminded Rostnikov of a small actor playing a businessman. Malenko was about sixty, with bushy grey-black hair and a determined, furrowed brow. It was a hard face, one that had suffered and worked, not the soft image of the black market capitalist that had flourished in Russian movies and posters during the two decades after the war. This did not surprise Rostnikov. What little he had been able to gather on Malenko told him that the man had begun humbly enough—a farmer's son and a farmer himself, who had gone to work in a tubing factory when he was thirty-five and made himself an expert on tubular metal construction. He used this expertise to move up in the factory at the same time as he moved up in party circles by applying himself diligently to political organization. Sergei Malenko was a clever man and not a weak one.

The room was very much the man, with well-polished, heavy wooden furniture, dark brown walls and rug, a fireplace already crackling with burning logs in spite of the fact that the house obviously had another heat source. On the walls were painted portraits of Lenin and figures unknown to Rostnikov.

"I'm sorry to be a bit abrupt, Inspector," Malenko said, sitting in a dark couch and indicating to Rostnikov that he should sit across from him in a matching couch, "but I do have to get to my work."

"I understand fully," said Rostnikov with an apologetic smile as he seated himself, letting his leg remain out where it would not stiffen.

"This is about Ilyusha," said the man, looking directly at Rostnikov, his hands folded before him. Malenko's suit was similar to Rostnikov's, but there were subtle differences. Malenko's was much newer, and he wore a light green sweater of some particularly soft material.

"It is about your son," Rostnikov confirmed.

"I imagine he is—" and it was Malenko's turn to be interrupted by his wife, who pushed open the door and moved forward quickly with a tray containing two steaming cups of coffee.

"You want sugar and milk?" Malenko asked, taking some himself.

Rostnikov declined. He assumed the coffee would be good and he had good coffee so infrequently that he wanted it to be very hot and its taste very distinct.

"You have some questions about Ilyusha?" Malenko asked after his wife had withdrawn from the room, closing the door behind her.

The coffee was good and very hot and very strong. It burned the roof of Rostnikov's mouth, and he wished he had asked for some milk.

"My first question is perhaps a bit tactless," he said. "If so, please forgive me." He put up his hands and shrugged in apology. "I'm a policeman and spend much of my time asking crude questions to enemies of the state and not to respected men of production. It strikes me as curious that a policeman comes to your house, that you know it concerns your son, and that you are not upon me with curiosity demanding to know if he is all right, what he has done. Instead you calmly drink your coffee and worry about getting to work."

"The question is tactless," agreed Malenko, "but reasonable. I have had little contact with my son for many years, perhaps four or five. We were never close. I think he took up with those dissenters, those social disrupters in reaction to me. And I suppose you are here to tell me that he has gotten into some trouble because of these stupid activities of his."

"In a sense," said Rostnikov. "Then, I take it, if your son were in trouble, it is not likely he would come to you for help."

Sergei Malenko began to laugh. He laughed so hard that the cup in his hand began to shake, and he just reached the dark mahogany table just in time to set it down. His hair tumbled over, and he began to choke on his laughter.

"You'll have to pardon me," he said trying to pull himself out of his reaction, "but the very idea of Ilya coming to me for anything is laughable don't you see?"

"Not in the least," said Rostnikov sipping his own coffee.

"I have a new life, a new wife, a small daughter. Ilya is not part of that life. He spent seven years making my existence miserable, causing me trouble. He lived here and went to school. He was terrible in school. He got into trouble. Drinking, girls, gambling. He more than embarrassed me. He very nearly ruined me, and you know what? I think that is what he wanted to do. I finally threw him out. That is when he became a political dissident. I am the last person he would come to for. help and the last person who would help him. You understand?"

"We want him because we have good reason to believe he murdered someone," said Rostnikov softly.

Sergei Malenko's face went white.

"No. That could ruin me," he said almost to himself.

"It won't do him much good either," added Rostnikov.

Malenko looked up sharply.

"You either fancy yourself a wit or are foolish," Malenko said between his teeth. "In either case, I suggest you tread softly, Inspector. Whom is he supposed to have murdered?"

"So far," sighed Rostnikov, "his wife, Aleksander Granovsky, and a cab driver."

The information struck Malenko like the blow of a tire iron. He sank back heavily and looked suddenly much older than his years.

"Is it possible," he said so softly that Rostnikov could barely hear him, "that he would go so far to ruin me?"

"It is possible," said Rostnikov, finishing his coffee. "It is also possible that his actions have little or nothing to do with you."

"Then why did he do this?" demanded Malenko, his hair falling over his brow as he reached forward to pound on the table.

"I thought you might have some idea," Rostnikov tried, "but I gather you have not, or the only one you have is of no great use to us. Did you know your son's wife?"

"I met her once," whispered Malenko, "on the street with him. She was a pretty girl who wanted to be friendly, but Ilya made a sarcastic comment and led her away."

"Comment?" tried Rostnikov shifting his leg weight.

"Personal, political," said Malenko. "Not relevant."

"Perhaps—"

"Not relevant," insisted Malenko, and Rostnikov

nodded his agreement, though he could guess the content of the brief meeting between father and son on the street.

"You have no idea of where he could be, who he could go to?"

"None," said Malenko. "We were never close. He no longer has the friends he had when he lived here. And before here we lived on a small farm beyond Kurkino. It has had two owners since."

"I see," said Rostnikov, rising slowly. "Then I believe that is all. Your first wife, Ilya's mother. She died?"

"No," said Malenko. His mind was elsewhere, planning his protection from his son's reputation, but he answered, "We were divorced three years ago."

"I see," said Rostnikov. "And where can I find her?"

"It will do you no good to find her," said Malenko, brushing his hair back with a broad brown hand. "She is in the Vilna Rehabilitation Institute."

"Perhaps I can see her there," said Rostnikov.

"You can see her if you insist," said Malenko, guiding the policeman to the hall and toward the door, "but she will provide you no information. She is quite mad. She hears and sees no one but whoever might exist within her head."

"I'm sorry," said Rostnikov.

"There is reason to be," Malenko said, opening the front door. Over his shoulder Rostnikov could see the second Mrs. Malenko looking apprehensively at them from what must have been the kitchen door. "Your records will show that she attained this ultimate escape after she murdered our infant son, Ilyusha's brother, for no reason that anyone ever discovered.''

"I—I'm sorry," Rostnikov repeated.

Malenko closed the door, and Rostnikov found himself facing his car and driver. He considered turning around and making another assault on Malenko. There was much to be said, much he might learn if he could get him to talk about his son, but it was likely he could not be goaded into such talk. Malenko was a shrewd man and one who very likely contributed to making those close to him go mad. But Rostnikov would not, could not accept the simple explanation for murder that one was mad, even madness had its own logic. Ilyusha Malenko had apparently murdered three people, and he had a reason for doing so. The reason might make little sense, but it was a reason, and if Rostnikov could figure out what that reason was, he might be able to anticipate the young man's next move.

"Sir," said the driver as Rostnikov got back into the rear of the car and closed the door.

"Back to Petrovka. Wait. No, the hospital. I want to stop by and see one of the inspectors.''

"Sergeant Karpo," supplied the driver, pulling away from the house.

"You are well-informed," said Rostnikov.

Sasha Tkach had been sitting in Inspector Rostnikov's office with a pad of lined paper in front of him and several sharpened pencils. He did not sit behind the desk because he did not know how Rostnikov would take it if he found a junior officer there. Sasha Tkach felt more comfortable working with Rostnikov than with any other senior investigator, but it was wise to be cautious and not overly familiar. There was too much to lose. So while he waited for reports on the telephone taps and hoped that Malenko would be spotted by a uniformed officer or that he would make some mistake, Tkach sat on the wrong side of the desk unable to put his feet under it, made notes, and tried to complete his report on the discovery of the body of Malenko's wife. That is what he did with the front of his consciousness. Deeper, but not much deeper, he wondered. One murder with a sickle, another with a hammer. Was the madman mocking the symbols of the Soviet Union? He was a dissident or a potential one. Was this some elaborate, ghastly joke? Then what about the cab driver? A broken vodka bottle didn't fit. It was too much to worry about.

Tkach had spent five hours at the desk, unwilling even to leave for a drink to have with his sandwich, afraid to tie up the phone with a call to check on Karpo's condition. It was shortly after two when the call came. It was Maxim, the expert who was monitoring all of the phone taps through a central unit he manned alone.

"I think we have something," Maxim said with great excitement. "A call a few minutes ago to one of the people being monitored. A young man's voice said only, 'Meet me at four at the spot where I broke the window.' "

"That was all?" asked Tkach.

"That was all."

"Can you play that part of the tape to me over the phone?"

"Yes," said Maxim. "Give me just a few seconds."

And, in fact, in no more than thirty seconds, Tkach

heard a hum and a voice repeating the words, "Meet me at four at the spot where I broke the window." Even with the distortion of the telephone line, Sasha recognized the voice of Ilyusha Malenko. He had not been sure that he would be able to do so, but as soon as he heard the first words he saw before him the young man and before the short sentence had ended, Sasha was again seeing the dangling body of the young woman.

"That's him," said Tkach. "Who was the call to?"

"Lvov, Simon Lvov."

Tkach hung up and considered his alternative. He could wait for Rostnikov and chance missing Lvov, or he could go on his own and, assuming Lvov had not yet left his apartment, follow the old man to his meeting. Since Sasha knew both Lvov and Malenko by sight, it seemed reasonable not to wait. He scribbled a message to Rostnikov on the lined sheet and hurried out the door.

Emil Karpo was awake but his eyes were closed. He was aware that someone stood next to his bed. He was also aware that it was Rostnikov. The slight drag of the leg had given the older man away. There was a low level of conversation in the twelve-man ward, but no noise.

"Inspector," said Karpo, opening his eyes.

"How do you assess your progress, Karpo?"

Something approaching a sad smile played on Rostnikov's face. His coat collar, the left side, was awkwardly tucked under while his right stuck out at an angle. He was, Karpo knew, not a man dedicated to appearances.

"My eyes were closed not because of particular pain," explained Karpo softly, "but because I am making all necessary efforts to allow my body to recover. I wish to get back to duty within a week."

"The possibility exists," said Rostnikov, sitting on the edge of the bed to ease the pressure on his leg, "that you will lose that arm."

"I do not intend for that to happen," said Karpo without emotion.

"Emil Karpo, you may have no choice," Rostnikov responded masking quite distinct emotion. "The doctors are not going to consult with you."

"It is out of the question," Karpo said.

"There have been one-armed inspectors," Rostnikov said, leaning over.

"That was during the war against the Germans, and only Baulfetroya in Kiev," said Karpo, closing his eyes.

"I'm glad you came up with that. I had no examples in mind," Rostnikov answered. The thought chain had struck like lightning. Kiev, where his son Iosef had been stationed. Now Afghanistan. The murder of one child and murder by another.

Karpo sensed the change in his visitor and opened his eyes to see Rostnikov looking at a spot of nothing on the brown woolen blanket.

"I'll not lose the arm," Karpo said. "You have work. I'll be all right."

"Are you dismissing me, Sergeant Karpo?" Rostnikov rallied.

"I am relieving you of responsibility," said Karpo.

"I accept," smiled Rostnikov.

"What has happened to Kroft?" Karpo added as Rostnikov rose to leave.

"Imprisoned. The trial will wait till you are well enough to testify. So the faster you recover, the faster you can return to battling enemies of the state like Kroft."

"He saved my life," said Karpo, his eyes closed again.

"So?"

"I think that might be taken into account."

"Do you want it to be? In another sense, you might not be here if it were not for him."

"It was not his fault that I got out of bed with a bad arm to pursue him. He could have waited another day or two," said Karpo. "He is a confusing criminal in some ways."

"I've seen many like him," said Rostnikov, "but he did tell me something that may help."

"In the Granovsky murder?" Karpo said, trying to reopen his eyes and failing.

"No, about the proper grip for a dead lift. Don't worry about it. I'll talk to you tomorrow."

By the time Rostnikov got back to his office in Petrovka, Tkach had been gone almost forty minutes. The young officer had been wise enough to put the time in the right-hand corner of the message. Rostnikov called Maxim and asked if there was any other information. He had the impulse to get back in his car and race to Lvov's apartment, but he checked himself. He could not really help. With his leg he was too slow and conspicuous to follow anyone around Moscow. Tkach would have to handle this himself.

At 5:15 a call came. Rostnikov then decided that he would have to tell Sarah that Iosef was in Afghanistan. It was her right to know and worry, and if he did not tell her and she found out that he knew all along, she would hold it against him. She would try not to, but it would be there. It had happened before for things of much less importance. The call had been brief. Colonel Drozhkin wanted to see him at K.G.B. headquarters at seven the following morning.

Tkach had arrived in front of Simon Lvov's apartment just in time. He had been standing in the doorway of an apartment building across the street from Lvov's for no more than five minutes when the figure of a tall old man in a long dark coat emerged. Although Tkach was more than one hundred yards from Lvov, the old man was unmistakable. His tall, stooped form and his thin face with horn-rimmed glasses were clear from the distance, and traffic was very light so that nothing stood in the way.

It seemed quite early to Tkach. Lvov was giving himself a full hour. The place must either be quite far, or Lvov was planning to make a stop first. It was also possible that Lvov, who had been a known dissident, was well aware of the possibility of his being followed and wanted to give himself ample time to lose his follower.

Keeping up with Lvov proved to be no great problem for Tkach, at least at first. Lvov boarded a bus and Tkach, his face covered as if to keep out the chill wind, boarded behind him. Lvov rode without looking about and got off not far from Red Square. The crowds were thick on the relatively pleasant sunny day, and Tkach had to close the distance between himself and the old man. In the crowd in front of the Lenin mausoleum, Tkach confused a pair of tall, dark clad figures before him but managed to select the right quarry with little trouble. Lvov walked slowly to the Lobnoye Mseto, the four-hundred-year-old white stone platform where the Tsars had performed their executions. From there Lvov crossed Kuibyshev Street and entered G.U.M., the State Department Store, the biggest and most crowded store in Moscow. In Stalin's day it had been a massive office building, but in 1953, with Stalin's departure, it had been returned to its commercial use, a huge department store with curved display windows on the main floor, many small shops and a massive press of 350,000 customers each day. Tkach muscled his way past afternoon tourists and old women with white babushkas to keep up with Lvov, who moved slowly but steadily through the crowds without really pausing to look in any windows.

It became clear to Tkach that the old man was diligently and intelligently trying to lose him. The moment of truth came at one of the first level overpasses between the store's sections. Lvov paused at the dark metal railing to look up at the arcade's glass ceiling several stories above. He seemed to be in no hurry. Tkach stopped and leaned against a wall on one side of the overpass. A crowd of people surged out of a store and moved onto the bridge toward Tkach, coming between himself and Lvov who remained along the rail and moved quickly to the other side. Tkach considered forcing his way over the overpass but realized that he would surely lose Lvov if he did so. The alternative was to anticipate where the old man was going. He could see Lvov's thin figure above the crowd moving away and Tkach guessed and acted. He went back into the store behind him, found the stairway and ran to the lower level. On the main floor of the arcade he ran through the window-shopping crowds and headed to the far exit. A tall, thin figure was just touching the bottom of the steps, and the panting Tkach slowed down for an instant, but only for an instant. The figure was not Lvov.

He looked around frantically and headed for the stairs pushing people out of the way. A very fat man said something in an angry hiss that might have been English, but Sasha didn't pause. He didn't even care now if he ran headlong into Lvov as long as he could catch sight of him, but he could not find the thin figure he sought.

There was no help for it. He would have to return to Petrovka and report to Rostnikov. He assumed the next step would be for Rostnikov himself to pay a visit to Lvov after Lvov's meeting with Malenko.

CHAPTER TEN

It was no more than two minutes after four when Simon Lvov returned to his apartment, the apartment where, no more than a month before, Ilyusha Malenko, quite drunk, had accidentally broken a window. Lvov had led the young policeman away, easily lost him, and had returned almost on the dot. He had left his door open and the lights off.

"Where were you?" Ilyusha Malenko's voice came from the corner near the window.

Lvov slowly took his coat off and hung it on a hook near the door.

"Ilyusha, my phone is probably monitored by both the police and the K.G.B." He moved slowly and wearily from his recent outing and sat in his chair. "I had to get them away from here, lose them."

"They are after me," Malenko said, stepping away from the window.

"I advise you to remain right where you were," said Lvov reaching for his pipe. "I shall leave the light off and we shall talk quickly. Then you shall leave. If you do not, they will surely catch you."

"You know why I'm here?" whispered Malenko from the dark.

"You killed Aleksander," said Lvov without looking back.

"Yes," replied Malenko, his voice quivering. "And I killed Marie too."

Lvov dropped his pipe and couldn't resist turning to the voice.

"You—"

"You know why," Malenko said. "You know why. You were part of it. Part of making a fool of me."

"Ilyusha . . ." Lvov began trying to get up but finding himself trembling.

"Don't say Ilyusha to me," Malenko's voice broke. "I trusted Aleksander. I trusted you, but you are no better than anyone else. No better than, than—"

"Your father?" Lvov supplied. "And Marie was no better than your mother?"

"Shut up," Malenko hissed, taking a step away from the dark shadow of the wall.

Lvov shook his head.

"So you've come to kill me?"

"Yes. I'll smash you. I'll smash all the liars and cheats who have made me into a fool. I'll not be a fool. You hear. I'll not be a fool."

"You came at the right moment," said Lvov, his voice regaining control. "I think I have no great interest in remaining alive. Had you come an hour later I might have struggled and argued and wept, but I don't want to argue with you. If you kill me it will be meaningless."

"It's not meaningless," cried Malenko taking another step forward. In his hand he held a scissors, a heavy pair of tailor's scissors. Lvov saw the object and choked back a sob of fear.

"No, it is not meaningless," he agreed. "You kill me and someone else and someone else and someone else till the police catch you. You know why you are doing this? Because it is over for you and you won't admit it to yourself. When you admit it to yourself you will stop running, stop killing, stop having meaning. You will be the nothing you fear you are."

"Shut up," shouted Malenko, raising his scissors.

"Rejoice not when thine enemy falleth, and let not thy heart be glad when he stumbleth, lest the Lord see it and it displeases Him and He turn away His wrath from him."

"What are you talking about?" Malenko cried, pausing.

"Proverbs 24:17-18," said Lvov. "I've been sitting in this room for years with nothing to do but listen to hopeful young men and read. In the process, I remembered that I am a Jew. When you forsake one God, the God of communism, or it forsakes you, you search for another. I have read the words, but I have not accepted them. I've lost my belief in anything and so have you, but I am an old man who needs no father and you are a young man lost in the wilderness."

"You're a crazy old man," Malenko whimpered, lowering his scissors still further.

"Maimonides said that when a man has a mean

opinion of himself, that any meanness he is guilty of does not seem outrageous to him. You've come to this state, Ilyusha. Killing me won't end it. I'll tell you the truth. You've heard it in my voice. I've pretended, but I'm afraid. But at the same time, I am not wrong. You can't get back what you lost, and you must accept that the meaning you have chosen will come to an end and leave you empty.''

''You are right,'' Malenko said. ''Of course. That is what I needed. I needed your advice. I can't erase it by destroying all of the ridiculing faces. I couldn't erase it by killing even my father. I must do to him what he did to me. I must balance the scales. His death and hers didn't balance the scales. It brought justice but it didn't balance the scale. Your death wouldn't balance the scale.''

The late afternoon had brought darkness, and out of it came Malenko's laughter.

''What will you do?'' asked Lvov, straining to see the outline of his visitor.

''It is not simple murder that will set me free of what he did to me,'' he said softly. ''Why didn't I see that? There was but one of her. There are two of them.''

And with that he went to the door and was gone.

Lvov knew that he had wet his pants and that his face was damp with tears. He pulled himself from his chair and went to the door, locking it. Then he hurried back to his heavy chair and slowly, slowly, slowly pushed it across the room against the door. When the chair was firmly in place, Simon Lvov took off his pants and underwear and started slowly across the room toward his dresser.

Out of the corner of his eye he saw a man in the room, and before fear could overtake him he realized that the man was his own reflection. He looked at his distorted image in the window glass. It was a ridiculous sight. A tall old man in a sweater wearing no pants and a little shriveled penis bobbing up and down. Lvov began to laugh. And then he began to cry, and had anyone been able to ask him at the moment if he were very happy or very sad he would have been totally unable to answer.

By the time he got to bed that night, Porfiry Rostnikov concluded that he had experienced far better days. Karpo was almost certainly going to lose his left arm. Malenko had been lost, lost by Tkach's inability to follow a nearsighted old man. In the morning he had to face Colonel Drozhkin at the K.G.B. The toilet was completely backed up, and while he was confident that he could repair it, he was aware that the part he needed might be almost impossible to obtain. That did not deter him. If necessary he would get a book on machine shop tools and learn to make the part. He was determined to absorb the totality of human knowledge if necessary to repair that toilet. But all this had been nothing compared to Sarah's reaction to his news about Iosef.

He had told her after dinner and she had taken it well, too well. All she had said was, "I see," and had gone back to watching television. It was a special film produced by the USSR Central Television and the Soviet Academy of Sciences. It was about Pavlov and showed the physiologist in his Leningrad research center while a voice told of his accomplishments. They both watched without speaking. They watched movies of H.G. Wells visiting Pavlov. They heard Pavlov speak about his concern with objective experimentation and the extension of conditioned reflex methodology to the problems of neurology and psychiatry. They watched and absorbed nothing. When it was over, Sarah had touched his hand and gone to bed two hours earlier than usual. Rostnikov had lifted weights for more than an hour till a tremor in the tendon of his weak leg warned him that he must stop. He defied the tendon, which knew more than he, concluded one more brief exercise, and then stopped. He took a cold shower, since there was no hot water, and tried to read an American paperback by a black writer named Chester Himes. It was about police in Harlem, New York, which struck Rostnikov as a mad, violent place. He prefered Isola or even Moscow.

The next morning he woke up early and touched Sarah, who slept soundly. She resisted, waking so he touched her again, and she sat up, turning on him.

"You don't have to break my arm," she shrieked.

"I just touched you," he said.

"I didn't sleep," she said, turning back into the bed.

"You slept soundly," he said, knowing he should simply stop but unable to do so.

"You sat up all night watching me sleep?" she asked with sarcasm.

"No," he said, moving to the sink to heat water so he could shave. "Forget it. You didn't sleep."

"Don't humor me," she said angrily. "You think I slept all night."

Rostnikov turned on the light in the corner. The sun

was not yet up out the window. He looked into the darkness outside and then at her.

"Iosef will be all right," he said.

"Now you're a god," she said, glaring at him.

"No. He will be all right."

Sarah looked at him for an instant and then turned her head away into her pillow. He finished his shaving, dressed, found some bread in the cupboard and a piece of cheese, and made himself a lunch, which he rolled in some newspaper and placed in his worn briefcase.

At the door he paused.

"Goodbye," he said.

"I'm sorry," she said.

He wanted to repeat that Iosef would be all right, but his mouth went dry and the words called him a liar. The *Volga* and the new driver were waiting for Rostnikov at the curb in front of his house. People hurrying to work in the near dawn glanced to see who was important enough in the neighborhood to merit a car and driver.

"Why are you here?" Rostnikov asked.

"Orders from the Procurator's office," he responded instantly. "I am to pick you up and be available throughout your current investigation."

"That will be most helpful, Michael Veselivitch Dolguruki," Rostnikov answered getting into the back seat.

"You remembered my name," said the driver, pulling into the nearly empty street.

"You are an unusually talkative driver," said Rostnikov.

"I'm sorry, comrade," answered the driver. "I assume that is a rebuke."

"Assume only that you made some impression on

me," said Rostnikov, looking out the window. "Do you know where the K.G.B. headquarters is?"

"Of course," said the driver.

"That is where we are going."

This time Rostnikov did not wait at all. He announced himself at the front desk, and seconds later the man named Zhenya appeared to lead him up to Colonel Drozhkin's office. Again, Rostnikov had to hurry behind him to keep pace.

"Go right in," said Zhenya.

"Thank you," replied Rostnikov, reaching down to massage his leg. Zhenya watched him for a second and then turned and left. Rostnikov knocked and entered the room before waiting for an answer.

"Rostnikov," said Drozhkin, without rising. Rostnikov decided that the colonel resembled the dead branch of a birch tree. The image pleased him and gave him a secret to sustain him through the conversation.

"I called you here to say that we appreciate the speed with which you conducted the Granovsky investigation," said Drozhkin, looking up with a pained look on his face that Rostnikov took to be a smile.

"Thank you, Colonel," said Rostnikov. He was not offered a seat, and Drozhkin seemed not to have noticed. Then the colonel realized the situation and said, "Please sit down."

Rostnikov sat and nothing was said for a few seconds.

"This Vonovich will be given a quick trial," Drozhkin said, fixing his eyes on Rostnikov, who returned the look while holding a gentle smile on his face.

"That," said Rostnikov, "is up to Procurator Timoteyeva."

"Of course," said Drozhkin, standing nervously. "I was not asking a question. I was making an observation. I understand that you are already on another murder, an entirely unrelated murder."

"I am on another murder," said Rostnikov.

Drozhkin paced to a corner nervously, looked out of the window behind him and turned to face Rostnikov with hands behind his back.

"Neither of us is a fool, Inspector."

"Yes, Colonel."

"Good," Drozhkin said, returning to his desk. "I understand that troops are being rotated in Afghanistan this very day. I know this because we have direct contact with agents who are there. We can get information and relay orders instantly. While our relations with the military have been strained in the past, this is a new era, especially where political matters are involved. It is hypothetical, of course, but we could have individual soldiers transferred or even recalled from the front if we thought it necessary."

"I see," sighed Rostnikov.

"Good," said Drozhkin. "Well, I hope you catch your new murderer as swiftly as you caught your last one. And I hope you will be hearing from your son very soon."

Drozhkin started to rise again but changed his mind, and Rostnikov moved slowly to the door.

"Thank you, Colonel," Rostnikov said.

The K.G.B. officer did not answer.

Zhenya was waiting outside the door to escort Rostnikov out, but Rostnikov had no intention of rushing after him. He walked slowly, and Zhenya was forced to stop and wait twice.

At the door, Rostnkov said "Thank you, comrade," to the retreating back of Zhenya and moved to the waiting car.

"Next time you wait for me," Rostnikov said, sinking back into the seat, "turn off the engine. You waste petrol."

"Yes, sir," said the driver.

A blanket of heat lay on Sonya Granovsky like a wet cat, as she tried to read by the light of the single bulb in the apartment on Dimitry Ulanov Street. She was as far from where her husband's body had been as she could be. The police had tried to keep her from returning, but she had threatened to go to the housing board. The apartment was hers. If they had completed their investigation, she wanted to return with her daughter. Apartments were not easy to get and she didn't want this one picked cold by some policeman who wanted to move his family in over the body of her husband. She would fight them at every step. She didn't know why the apartment was so warm. Perhaps it wasn't warm at all. Perhaps she was feverish. It was possible.

It was almost dawn. In the hall two tenants were arguing about something. She could make out few of their words and didn't want to listen to them. She had been unable to sleep. In the other room, her daughter Natasha lay dreaming fitfully, tossing and moaning. There was nothing Sonya wanted to do, but what she wanted least was to sit alone in that smothering dark room. It had, she admitted, been terrible here when Aleksander was alive. They had never been happy and she had never liked him, though she had loved him and respected him. He had provided the focus of meaning in her life. She knew no other.

The voices in the hall grew louder, a man and a woman. It had something to do with using hot water. Sonya wanted to go to the door and shout at them to be quiet, but she couldn't bear to be part of what would follow such an act. She couldn't rise. Moist hands of heat pushed her down trickling wet under her print dress, between her breasts and thighs, into the hair between her legs, making her shudder and whimper. She closed her eyes again and opened them to her daughter standing in the door to the second room.

"What's the noise?" she asked sleepily.

Sonya thought there was contempt in the girl's eyes as she looked down at her, as if she knew her thoughts and feelings, as if she probed her mind and body and shame. Sonya had seen this look in Aleksander's eyes.

"Just some neighbors fighting, arguing," Sonya said. "Go back to sleep for a while. Are you warm?"

Natasha, whose hair was wound in braids, was wearing long-sleeved flannel pajamas that had been Sonya's.

"No," said the girl, heading back into the dark room.

The fight stopped abruptly in the hall, and a door closed. Footsteps went down the corridor, and there was silence. Sonya pushed herself from the chair, her back soaked with sweat and her bare lower legs sticky. The wooden floor boards creaked when she crossed the room and went to look out the window into near darkness.

The knock at the door was firm and insistent. Sonya

started and wasn't sure that it had been a real sound and not just something in her head. Then it came again.

"Coming," she said. It was probably her brother Nikolai, stopping to see her on the way to work.

Before opening the door, Sonya paused at the wall to look at the photograph of her and Aleksander on the day of their wedding. She knew that it would soon become a ritual, a requirement. She would have to look at the photograph every time she passed. There were no words to give to this sensation, but it was welling in her nonetheless.

Sonya opened the door, not to the pale sad face of her brother, but to the figure of a young man in a black coat.

"Ilyusha," she said softly. "What are you doing here?"

He moved quickly past her.

"Is Natasha here?" he said, looking around.

"Yes," Sonya said confused. "What is wrong?"

He paused for a moment and looked at her. He looked as if he had not slept in days. Certainly he had not shaved.

"Don't you know about Marie?" he asked, his hands plunged deeply into his pockets.

"Marie? No. What?"

"She's dead," he said, taking a step toward her. Sonya Granovsky stepped back.

"Dead?"

"Dead, dead, dead," he repeated. "And so is Aleksander."

"I know," said Sonya softly. "Please, Ilyusha, sit down. I'll make some tea and we'll talk." She moved toward the kettle, but Malenko stepped in her way.

"Do you know who killed Aleksander?" he whispered.

"A man named Vonovich," she said. "I know you're upset Ilyusha, but you've got to keep quiet. Natasha is sleeping. It's been very hard for her."

Malenko shook his head and ran his hand through his hair.

"Hard for her," he chuckled.

"Ilyusha, are you sure Marie is dead?" Sonya Granovsky said softly. "Maybe you're just upset by what happened to Aleksander and—"

Ilyusha Malenko's sudden move forward sent her staggering back. Panic was in his eyes.

"Oh no," he said, holding his hand out while the other remained in his coat pocket. "That's what happened before. I wasn't sure what had happened, but I proved it with the cab driver. I proved it. It did happen. She is dead. I hit her and hung her up. I killed her and the cab driver and Alek. I did. You aren't going to convince me that I didn't."

His hand came out of his pocket slowly, holding a large, heavy pair of rusty scissors.

"Ilyusha," Sonya started to scream.

"But it's not enough," he said, stepping toward her. "Simon convinced me, showed me, it's not enough. He's the one I should have listened to all the time. I'm going to make things even."

Sonya was paralyzed with fear. She imagined herself turning to run, feeling the thud of a heavy blow to her back, and knowing that filthy thing in his hand was plunging into her. There was nowhere to run. She stood in confusion and terror as he moved to her.

"I'll explain," he said, holding his free hand up to his lips. "Let's be quiet and not wake Natasha yet. I'll explain and you'll understand why I will do what I must do."

At the moment Ilyusha Malenko had entered the Granovsky apartment on Dimitry Ulanov Street, Porfiry Rostnikov was on his way back to his office from his meeting with Colonel Drozhkin. He weighed in his mind the possibility of trading what he knew for the safety of his son. The deliberation was brief. He would do what he could to protect Iosef. He would trade with the odious colonel. What difference did it make if Malenko went to Siberia for killing his wife or for killing Granovsky and the cab driver too? The K.G.B. wanted it finished so the political crisis could end. Then so be it, it was ended. Of course it meant that Vonovich would go to trial and be quickly convicted of murders he did not commit, but Rostnikov was also convinced that Vonovich had murdered some unknown human in his past. It didn't matter to Rostnikov who murdered whom as long as the killers were all caught, stopped, and punished. What nagged Rostnikov was something much more basic than that. The "who" was no longer important. What was important was "why."

"Wait," he called to the driver as they turned down the street less than a block from Petrovka. "We have someplace else to go."

The driver made a broad U-turn and headed back where he was told without comment. There was no time to waste. Rostnikov would confront Lvov directly and see what he could discover. Tkach had had two

176

chances, but there was a limit to the amount of time he could give the young man when the issues were so important. There was a chance, Rostnikov realized, that he had given Tkach too much authority, had relied too heavily on him, had treated him and viewed him as a substitute son, a hedge against the possible loss of Iosef. If it were true, it may have jeopardized this investigation, for Tkach was not yet worthy of the responsibility he had been given.

When they pulled up to the apartment building where Simon Lvov lived, Rostnikov told the driver to turn off the engine.

It was easy to find the apartment of Simon Lvov. What proved to be more difficult was getting the old man to open the door.

"Lvov," Rostnikov shouted, after knocking loudly. "I can hear you in there. This is the police. I'll give you fifteen seconds to open the door, and then I call my man in to shoot it down." Rostnikov knew he would do nothing of the kind, but he was not worried about losing face in front of this old dissident who had some information he might be able to use.

"You have ten seconds," he said, not knowing if five, ten, or thirty seconds had passed.

Behind the door he could hear the shuffling of furniture, something heavy being moved and then the padding of footsteps to the door. A chain was pulled and a latch thrown before the door creaked open.

Rostnikov pushed his way in and turned on the tall, thin grey man in a worn purple robe that failed to cover his white boney knees.

"You are Simon Lvov?" Rostnikov barked.

"Yes, I . . ."

"I am Chief Inspector Rostnikov. You will sit, and I will sit, and you will answer some questions."

Lvov sat dutifully across from the policeman, who stared at him. Rostnikov felt a stirring in him to back off. The old man before him was a pathetic, drifting creature, showing none of the elusiveness of tongue or mind that Tkach had reported. Either something had changed him, or Tkach had badly misjudged the man, which was unlikely.

"What did Malenko tell you?" he asked.

"Malenko?"

"Ilyusha Malenko. You saw him, met him. You know where he is hiding, what he is going to do. You can be put on trial for aiding a murderer."

Lvov pushed his glasses back on his nose, and a spasm rippled across his face.

"He was going to kill me," Lvov said. "I thought I didn't care, but when the moment came, I cared very much."

"What did he say? Why didn't he kill you? Where is he?"

"I don't know," said the old man. "He said he had to even things with Granovsky. That killing me would not do it."

"Even things?" Rostnikov asked. "What quarrel did he have with Granovsky?"

"I don't know," said Lvov. "They were friends, more like—I don't know. Ilyusha worshiped Alek, would have done anything for him. Then this."

"There has to be a reason," Rostnikov insisted. "Why kill his friend and his own wife? Why—was there something between Granovsky and Malenko's wife?'' The idea seemed obvious and yet elusive. It depended totally on the association of the two murders for a motive. It meant, as Rostnikov was certain anyway, that Malenko was the sole murderer.

"Perhaps," shrugged Lvov.

"Only perhaps?"

"It is quite likely," said Lvov quietly. "Aleksander was an articulate and brave leader, but he was in many ways less than an honorable man."

"It makes no sense," said Rostnikov almost to himself. "If he caught them, why didn't he kill them together, or her first? If she confessed, why did he kill Granovsky first? You see?"

"No," said Lvov, who clearly did not see.

"Who told him about his wife and Granovsky, the man he worshipped like a father?"

"I don't know," said Lvov. "Would you like some tea?"

"No," mused Rostnikov. "He said he had to make it even. That there were two of them. Perhaps he means to murder his father and stepmother."

"Perhaps," agreed Lvov, rising and moving slowly across the floor on thin white legs to prepare some tea.

"Two of them," Rostnikov repeated and then the image came into his mind. It was a pair of thin shadows, and then the light touched them, and they had faces and the faces were those of Sonya and Natasha Granovsky.

He was back in the car in less than twenty seconds. The driver started the engine as soon as Rostnikov got in and shouted for him to hurry to Dimitry Ulanov Drive.

The driver turned as if to speak, saw Rostnikov's pale face, and said nothing.

"Hurry, hurry," urged the police inspector, and the driver hurried.

He was the best driver Rostnikov had ever seen. They took corners, even still icy ones, without a skid and without a slowdown. His hands remained steady and he anticipated lights and pedestrians as he sped through the streets. The trip took no more than ten minutes.

"Listen," he told the driver as he got out. "We are looking for a man named Malenko, Ilyusha Malenko. He is twenty-eight and probably wearing a black coat. You don't let anyone out of that door who even vaguely might be Malenko. You understand?"

"I understand," the driver said, getting out and unbuttoning his holster.

"Good. I think he has killed three people and is quite dangerous. I would like him alive, but if that is not possible . . . You understand."

Rostnikov hurried into the hall and to the elevator, but a sign was hung on it, indicating that it was out of order. Rostnikov began the climb up the stairs. He tried to hurry, but his leg denied him. At the third floor, he had to rest. Two young teen-age boys hurried past the exhausted man and fell into silence until they were a floor below him, where they said something about him being drunk. Rostnikov forced himself up. By the sixth floor he was in pain and dragging his foot. It struck him only then that he had no gun with him. He seldom used one. It was not that he was against the use of weapons, but the need came up so seldom that he left his gun locked in a drawer in his office.

There was no time to worry about it. He plunged down the hall, found the door, and knocked.

"Mrs. Granovsky. Sonya Granovsky," he cried.

There was no answer. Rostnikov wasn't sure of how strong the door was. In truth, at the moment, he wasn't sure of how strong he was, but he planned to try. There was little room in the narrow corridor. He pushed himself against the wall opposite the door, placed his palms against the wall behind him, braced his bad foot and lifted his good one for a kick. He had taken two deep breaths and was about to kick, when he heard something behind the door. A movement. Something. He hesitated, stood up, and leaned forward to listen.

"Is someone in there?" he called. Silence. "Is someone in there?"

The door began to open, and the face of Sonya Granovsky appeared.

"Yes?" she said.

"It is me, Inspector Rostnikov. You remember me from the other night?"

"I remember you." She looked thin and ill, as if she were about to collapse.

"May I come in?" he asked gently.

"No," she said. "I'm afraid I . . ."

"I'll have to insist," he said as kindly as he could. She backed away and he entered carefully, ready.

"Where is your daughter?" he asked.

"Sleeping in the next room," she said, folding her hands over her thin breasts and hugging herself as she sat in a wooden chair and failed to meet his eyes. There was something like the attitude of Simon Lvov about her.

"Late to be sleeping, isn't it?" he asked, taking a

step toward the closed door.

Sonya Granovsky stood up quickly and nervously, her right hand out to stop him.

"No," she said, her voice breaking. "She's been upset since . . . all this. Please let her sleep."

Rostnikov turned from the door and supported himself on the edge of the sofa where he had first seen the two women. If something was in that room with which he had to deal, it would be best dealt with when his strength returned.

"Have you seen Ilyusha Malenko recently?" Rostnikov tried.

Sonya Granovsky collapsed back into the chair as if he had slapped her. Her head shook fiercely.

"No, no, no," she said, without looking up.

"You have seen him," Rostnikov repeated. "And you know what he has done."

"No," she cried. "No."

"What is wrong here?" Rostnikov whispered moving away from the sofa toward the trembling woman. "Is he in there with your daughter?"

Her head shook violently to deny it, but Rostnikov could take no more. He looked around for a weapon, settled for one of the wooden chairs, picked it up easily, and limped to the closed door.

"No," whimpered Sonya Granovsky, but Rostnikov did not hesitate. He threw his shoulder into the door, hoping that Malenko was right behind it listening and would be taken by surprise. The surprise was Rostnikov's. He hurtled into the room and rolled onto the bed and against the wall. He righted himself as quickly as he could, prepared for an attack but nothing came. Sunlight came through the window, and he could see no one but himself in a wall mirror, looking foolish on the floor with a chair cradled in his arms. He pulled himself up as Sonya Granovsky entered the room.

"Where is your daughter, Sonya Granovsky?" he demanded.

"He took her," she said.

CHAPTER ELEVEN

Viktor Shishko sat at his German-made typewriter in the office of the Moscow *Pravda,* turning the bit of information given him by Comrade Ivanov into a story. It was an important story dealing with the swift apprehension of the killer of Aleksander Granovsky. Viktor Shishko had been a reporter in Moscow for more than thirty years and had covered only two murder stories. He was well aware that dozens of murders took place every day in and around Moscow, but few of them were made known to anyone but the police and the people involved. Occasionally, though, there was a purpose to be served by publicity. Viktor Shishko found it easy to guess what the purpose was in this case, but he had no intention of sharing his conjecture with anyone else. When the story was finished, he would read it to Comrade Ivanov, who in turn would read it to someone who served the Party as liaison with the several investigatory agencies. Viktor had been through it all before and knew that the story would come back with small changes, cautious wording, though he himself was doing his best to be careful and anticipate the reason for the publication of the story.

Other writers, editors, and staff people, men and women, bustled past Viktor as he composed his short story:

Aleksander Granovsky, 42, former professor of history at Moscow University, was murdered last night by a cab driver with whom he had frequently quarreled. The cab driver, Mikel Vonovich, 39, wounded a police officer attempting to apprehend him. Trial will be held on the sixth of the month.

Shishko examined his brief story with satisfaction. He had omitted Granovsky's reputation as a dissident and the fact that Granovsky was due to go on trial the morning after his death. He had also moved the date of Granovsky's murder up one day to show how swiftly the police had caught the murderer. As an extra precaution, he had not included information about Vonovich's black market activity. It was not his function to anticipate the political consequences of such things. Therefore, he did not include them. If the party liaison wanted those things in for good reason, then he or she could put them in.

As for the rest—the shooting of the young man in the liquor store by Sasha Tkach; the shooting of the police officer by the dead boy; Emil Karpo's arm; Malenko's murder of his wife and a cab driver and the kidnapping of the dissident's daughter—Viktor Shishko knew nothing. And neither, therefore, would the people of Moscow.

Dark clouds had come back over Moscow, promising more snow. Through Anna Timofeyeva's window, Rostnikov watched the clouds push their way in front of the feeble sun. Rostnikov was in a bad mood.

"And?" asked Procurator Timofeyeva, looking particularly dyspeptic.

"And, Ilyusha Malenko attempted to rape Sonya Granovsky," he said.

"Attempted?"

"He was unable to do so."

"She resisted?"

"No, she agreed to be quiet so as not to disturb her daughter sleeping in the next room, but Malenko could not consummate the action," Rostnikov said carefully. He had no idea what Procurator Timofeyeva thought about sex as a personal act or a potentially criminal one. Surely, she had been involved in enough cases to have an opinion.

"Then?"

"Yes, then," Rostnikov went on, "he got angry. He went in and got the girl and said he was taking her with him. That he would be back for the mother when he had given the daughter what justice demanded."

"How old is the girl?" Timofeyeva asked, looking down at her notes for an answer.

"Fourteen," said Rostnikov. "Sonya Granovsky was told that if she mentioned what had happened, he would kill the girl, which he probably intends to do anyway."

"But he might not?"

"He might not," Rostnikov agreed.

There was silence in the room for a few seconds and then the distant rumbling of thunder. The room had grown quite dark, and Anna Timofeyeva rose to turn on the lights.

"And Malenko said to her that he had killed her husband?"

"That is what he said."

"He could have been lying," she went on, moving to her desk again. "He knew Granovsky was dead. He had killed his wife."

"Possible, of course," agreed Rostnikov. "Perhaps when we find him we can discover more."

"Awkward, very awkward," Anna Timofeyeva said between clenched teeth. Her breathing was heavy now, troubled. "What are you doing to find him?"

"We are trying to find out how he could get wherever he is through the streets of Moscow holding a crying young girl at the point of a scissors without anyone noticing."

"He had an accomplice," tried the procurator, opening her desk drawer to search for something. She found a small bottle of pills Rostnikov had never seen.

"Possible again, but not likely. It is more reasonable to suppose that he has also kidnapped the driver of a car, has stolen a car or has taken a cab and convinced the driver that nothing was amiss. I have some men checking on cabs, seeing if any cars have been reported missing. If he kidnapped a driver, it might be tomorrow before we find out about it if a relative calls the person in as missing."

"And meanwhile?" asked Timofeyeva, gulping down two white pills and ignoring Rostnikov's look of sympathy.

"I have a man guarding Sonya Granovsky's apartment, another man watching the house of Malenko's father. I've taken the liberty of doing all of this in your name, comrade."

She waved a thick hand to indicate that it was, of course, all right to do so.

"The Procurator General is almost at the end of his term," said Anna Timofeyeva softly. "Did you know that, Porfiry?"

"I was aware," he said. He wondered if the pills she had taken were for pain and, if so, if they would help to relieve the agony in his leg. The run up the stairs to the Granovsky apartment would be something to regret for days, maybe long enough to ruin his training and end any hope of the park competition.

"He would like to be reappointed," she went on. "It would be unprecedented to have such a second appointment. It would be very much to my advantage to have him reappointed, Porfiry. And if it is to my advantage, it is to yours. Do you understand?"

"I am to be discreet about my investigation," he said.

"I needn't tell you that my interests are not selfish," she said, rubbing the bridge of her nose, an act which, Rostnikov noticed, she did more and more frequently. "The Procurator is a good man, a good Party member, a just man. If he remains in office, we can continue our work as we have."

"It will be borne in mind."

"Go, Porfiry, and report to me when you know anything, anything at all. I will be right here through the night. And one more thing."

"Yes," grunted Rostnikov as he forced himself out of the chair.

"I would prefer that you reserve your maudlin sympathy when you come in here. Some might find it touching, but I find your concern merely burdensome. For example, I have of course noticed the extreme pain you are in from your leg. But my feeling about it must be put aside for the sake of our efficient functioning. We have tasks which must come before human weakness. We have goals for a better future."

"I agree," said Rostnikov, limping to the door.

"As soon as you hear anything," she said, pulling a thick folder in front of her.

Rostnikov went out the door thinking that Anna Timofeyeva and Sergei Malenko represented perfectly opposing wills. Malenko was a successful capitalist within a socialist country. He was the living evidence, an alternative, a corrupt alternative, perhaps, but one which refused to go away. Anna Timofeyeva labored for a utopia free of Malenkos, elder and younger, free of dissent, free of poverty. In his deepest heart, Rostnikov was confident that neither her world nor the world of Sergei Malenko would ever triumph. No utopia had ever survived; perhaps none was desirable. Man had evolved into a creature who lived in constant tension. Utopias might destroy him. And besides, in a perfect world there would be no room for the police.

It took forever to get back to his own office, where Sasha Tkach sat, his hair disheveled, his coat open. The young man slumped in the chair across the desk and didn't even fully turn to face Rostnikov.

"Any news from the cab investigation?" Rostnikov asked, easing himself into his chair and feeling the pain rush through his leg as he changed position. Rostnikov wondered if the German who had shot him in 1941 was still alive somewhere and if the German was walking on two whole legs. Rostnikov did not like Germans, even East Germans. They weren't to be trusted.

"Nothing," said Tkach.

"Stolen cars, kidnappings, missing persons?"

"Nothing," said Tkach, looking down at his thumbs. Rostnikov leaned over to see what was so interesting about Tkach's thumbs, but could see nothing.

"You have something on your mind, Sasha," Rostnikov sighed.

"I think I should be given . . . I should have less responsible assignments until I can prove myself," he said. "I've bungled all of this badly."

"You have," agreed Rostnikov. "To use the terms of hockey, you have allowed as many goals as you have scored."

"Yes. Had I remembered that the cab driver had been killed near Petro Street, I could have prevented the murder of Marie Malenko. Had I not lost Simon Lvov, he would have led me to Ilyusha Malenko and he would not have kidnapped the girl."

"I know," said Rostnikov. Tkach looked at him, waiting for further comment.

"Is that all you can say?" asked Tkach more in a plea than anger.

"What more can I say? You made mistakes. I am not your father. I can't forgive you for your mistakes, neither will I sit here brooding on them. You have a job. You do it. Sometimes things go right. Sometimes they go wrong. If we demoted every police officer who made major mistakes, there would be no senior officers left. You have many inadequacies as an investigator, Sasha, perhaps even more than I, but I think, frankly, that we are the best available. So let's stop worrying about the past and start considering the present and future. Let's begin by your getting me half a dozen aspirin and a pot of tea."

Something approaching a smile touched Sasha Tkach's mouth and he brushed back his hair.

"I haven't given you a reprieve," said Rostnikov, rubbing his leg, "only a minor task. Please do it."

Gas is not easy to get in Moscow, which is one of the reasons so few Muscovites own automobiles. But there are many other reasons. Automobiles are very expensive and the laws governing their use are many. But the worst thing about owning an automobile in Moscow is the repairs. There are less than a dozen shops in Moscow authorized to repair automobiles. Working in these shops are mechanics who frequently resent the fact that they must work on these automobiles without any prospect of ever owning one themselves. Parts are difficult to get and repair work is usually done quickly and badly. The mechanics get paid the same for good or bad work, and the customers really have no choice.

Vera Alleyenovskya, a second cellist in the Bolshoi theater orchestra, was a near tireless perfectionist; her only indulgence was the automobile. Her *Volga* had been repaired four times in the last month only to develop the same problem anew each time. And each time she had patiently returned it for repair. The car spent more days in the shop that month than on the road. Vera Alleyenovskya was beginning to consider getting rid of the car. This thought was connected in her mind with the possibility of accepting the offer of marriage of Igor Petschensky, the tuba player. Both would involve a radical change in self-image for which she was preparing herself.

Vera Alleyenovskya looked at herself in the rearview mirror when she got into her car, which had now been running for two days without a breakdown. Her blond hair was tied straight back, her eyes were blue, her skin clear and pale, her face a bit chunky. At moments like this, she tended to push the sale of the car and the proposal of Petschensky deep into the recesses of her mind. After all, it was one thing to deal with a tuba as part of the total sound of the Rimsky-Korsikov, but to hear the individual rehearsal might be too much in spite of Petchensky's admirable mustache. Vera Alleyenovskya saw something else in her mirror this evening, and it was to have a profound effect on her life.

In the mirror was the face of a young man. Vera Alleyenovskya turned quickly with a half scream.

"No," said the young man, showing a long, rusty scissors and glancing out of the window to see if any passerby noticed what was happening inside the parked car. Then Vera Alleyenovskya saw the young girl. The man had one arm around her, holding her mouth. The girl's eyes were wide and frightened.

"What do you want?" asked Vera quietly. "What are you doing in my car? With that child?"

"I want you to turn around and start the car," Ilyusha Malenko said. "Now. I can easily kill you and drive myself, but then I'd have to do something with little Natasha here and I don't want anything to happen to her, not now. So drive."

Vera Alleyenovskya drove. She had no idea of who the young man was. Her primary source of information was the Moscow *Pravda*.

"We're cold," said the young man, looking over her shoulder into traffic. "We've been sitting in here on the floor for hours. Turn on the heat."

"It takes a while to work," Vera said. "Where shall I take you?"

"Later," he said, tapping her on the shoulder with the scissors. "Later. And don't think clever thoughts. I am clever too, and I have grown quite used to doing what I must. There are three dead to prove it."

The young man sounded proud of his accomplishment. A look in the rearview mirror at both him and the girl seemed to support what should have been a confession but sounded like a boast.

"I do not have an inexhaustable supply of petrol," Vera said, driving through the new falling snow.

"Later," he growled. "How do you come to own a car?"

"I'm a musician," Vera explained.

"My father owns two cars and a woman."

Vera had nothing to say. She nodded and drove.

"Drive out of the city," he said a few minutes later. Then to the young girl beside him. "I'm going to let you go. My hand is tired of holding you. You are to sit back in the corner and say nothing and not whimper. You understand?''

Vera couldn't see if the girl nodded, but she did hear a sudden gasp for air and the young girl's lungs taking in air loudly and quickly.

Vera drove along the highway past apartments and houses for almost an hour.

"Turn here," he ordered at one point, and she skidded, almost missing the road where he told her to turn. "Now drive."

Vera drove down the small highway for ten minutes and then the blades of the scissors clicked in the air near her cheek.

"There, there, there up ahead, turn into that road," said the young man.

She turned. The road was small and unpaved; the snow was piling up quickly.

"We can't go far," she said. "Too much snow. I should try to turn back."

"Never mind," said the young man. "Just get out. Leave the key and get out.

"Wait," she tried.

"Out," he shouted and Vera got out.

Her hope now was that this madman would simply abandon her and take the car. It had been a long while since they passed anything that looked like a house, and it was possible that any house she found now would not have a phone, but still it would mean safety. Her hope was short-lived. The young man stepped out of the back of the car, closing it behind him.

"You are going to leave me here?" Vera said firmly.

"Yes," he said, stepping toward her in the thick snow at the side of the road.

"Then I'll start walking," she said, backing away.

The white snow now mixed into the hair of the young man and stuck to his eyebrows and face. His head was nodding slowly.

"You'll tell the police," he said. "I can't have that."

"Why should I tell the police?" Vera said, taking another step back and almost falling.

"Because you would be a fool not to," he said reasonably.

"Now, wait . . ." Vera began taking a step toward Ilyusha with her hands out as if she were going to plead with him. He put his hands to his sides to let her come near, and shifted the scissors in his grip. The handle was cold and solid. He was ready, but not for what happened. Vera Alleyenovskya did not plead or beg or whimper. It was simply not in her to do so. Instead she threw her one hundred thirty pounds at the young man with her hands extended. He slid in the snow and stumbled backward against the car, and she turned to run toward a clumb of fir trees about fifty yards away across an open field. She could hear him get up behind her as she moved against the resistance of the accumulated snow, and after twenty yards she knew he was coming. Twenty yards further he had narrowed the gap, and just as she was about to touch the first birch tree, she could clearly hear two things: the heavy close footsteps of the man behind her and the opening of her car door.

She kept going, and heard the steps stop abruptly

behind her. Panting, the cold air burning her lungs, she leaned against a tree and looked back. The young man was racing back-across the field. Through the snow she could see the young girl standing indecisively next to the car, unsure of which way to run. She took a step back down the road and then considered going the other way. It was clear to Vera that the girl had neither the stamina nor will to get away from the young man, but she herself was now confident of survival. She took a deep, cold breath, warmed her mittened hands under her armpits and plunged through the trees.

Ilyusha caught Natasha Granovsky no more than ten feet from the car. He had to hold her for five minutes before he could either catch his breath or speak. Only then did he force her back into the car. He drove slowly, the girl at his side, the scissors in his hand as he gripped the steering wheel. In five minutes, he could drive no further. The road was too little and the snow too much.

"Out," he ordered. She was wearing boots, coat, and a warm hat and he a jacket. He pulled his scarf from his neck and tied it over his head and ears.

"That way," he ordered, pointing down the road with his scissors.

In ten minutes, the snow stopped and the moon came out. They walked. As steadily as the moon would guide him, they walked along the side of the road through the trees. Ilyusha led the way, feeling the chill patiently taking over his body. Behind him he could hear the light steps of the girl, who walked on numbly, allowing herself an occassional sob.

In Ilyusha's mind was a crude map almost eighteen

years old. He had no idea whether he would reach his goal, or die in the snow.

They were a pitiful sight against the sky, the one lean figure in front, a scarf around his head, and a thin figure in back, stumbling. Ilyusha was muttering and lurched forward, step after step, the scissors clinking open and closed in his hand and echoing through the trees.

When they broke through the woods into an open field, Natasha sagged against a birch tree, and Ilyusha was forced to abandon his reverie and turn his attention to the girl.

"I think we're getting near," he told her. "We'll find a place to sleep."

Ilyusha led the way again for twenty minutes until they found a small, darkened farm. They crept to a low barn and crawled through a wooden door. A cow snorted and rustled, ignoring the two intruders who fell heavily against the cold stone wall.

Ilyusha's eyes adjusted to the dimness, and he could make out the cow, the walls, a small window, and finally the girl, who lay next to him with eyes open, afraid to sleep. She looked feverish to Ilyusha.

"You're sick," he whispered.

"Because of you," she cried.

"I'm doing what I must," he said. "In the morning maybe I'll milk the cow for you. Sleep. I won't hurt you."

Inside Ilyusha, vying with the bloody face of the cab driver on Petro street, was the vision of himself and the girl making their way to his destination. He would steal something to eat in the morning early and get going. Ilyusha fought down the image of his wife Marie dangling in their apartment, her face . . .

Suddenly, he did not want to die. He sat up quickly and looked around, afraid. The small barn threatened to grow large. He could kill the girl, that might stop the barn from growing, but then he would be alone and he did not want to be alone. The sound of the cow and the steady breathing of the girl soothed and blanketed his thoughts. He lay back and slept but did not dream.

With first light, the barn door flew open and so did Ilyusha's eyes. The boy who looked at him was frightened, and for a moment Ilyusha did not know where he was. He had the feeling that the boy was himself eighteen years earlier, that he was looking at himself.

The boy stopped and turned.

"My name is Ilyusha," Ilyusha shouted, and Natasha sat up suddenly. "This is my sister. Our automobile got stuck on the road last night, and we wandered in here."

The boy stood about a step outside, framed in the sunlight and snow. Ilyusha made no move to rise and frighten him. He tucked the scissors carefully into his pocket and kept his hand on it. The boy's black eyes were curious and traveled from the voice in the darkness of the small barn to the safety of his own house behind him.

"My sister is ill," Ilyusha said softly. "We would be grateful for some water and maybe some bread."

The boy turned and ran into the house. Ilyusha reached down and forced the girl up. She was dazed and ill, a weight without thought.

"Say nothing or you die," he whispered. "You know I'll do it."

Ilyusha prodded her toward the door and looked back

at the cow. The cow, he could see, had some kind of growth near its udder and Ilyusha shuddered, thinking that he had considered touching and taking milk from the animal. The world was indeed rotten.

The madman and the girl stood stiffly in the morning cold and sun. They turned to face the house and the voices inside. From the farmhouse, a one-story mud and wood building tilted slightly to the west from age, the boy and a man came out. The man held an axe. He was lean and wearing a cowhide jacket. His face was bearded and dark, and he did not squint into the sun.

"We're from Moscow," Ilyusha explained. "We're on our way to visit relatives."

"Come into the house," the man said nodding his head. The little boy stepped back and allowed Ilyusha and Natasha to step in ahead of him. The lean man held tightly to his axe as he followed, watching them. The girl stumbled and Ilyusha led her to a chair where he took a position behind her.

The room was dark in spite of the windows letting in the morning light. A bed stood in the middle of the room against the wall, and on the bed lay a thin woman looking at them. Next to the bed was a set of crutches.

"My wife," explained the man, putting his axe against the wall but staying near as he ordered his son to pour tea for the two young visitors. The woman on the bed did not speak or move. She watched Ilyusha for a second and then fixed her eyes on Natasha Granovsky. Then she turned to the window, where her eyes remained.

"You can have some tea and bread," said the man. "We haven't much at the moment."

"We are grateful for whatever you can share with us, and I'm sure—"

"Are they coming here?" the man interrupted.

"Who?" asked Ilyusha, starting to pull out his scissor, trying to determine if he could get to the man before the man reached the axe.

"Whoever is after you. The girl's parents, brothers?"

"I—" began Ilyusha.

"When you finish, you leave," said the man, gesturing to the boy, who hurried to refill the visitors' cups with tea.

They ate in silence and rose.

Ilyusha asked the man if he was on the right road to his destination. The man replied that he was.

"In an hour, maybe less if the road is clear, you'll come to Nartchev Road. Take it left."

"We thank you," said Ilyusha, taking the girl's arm and leading her out the door. The boy and man remained inside. He urged the girl to hurry. When they reached the road, Ilyusha goaded her into a trot. He began to smile again. The sun was out, and he knew where he was going.

CHAPTER TWELVE

The night had been long for Rostnikov and Tkach as they dozed in his office. However, Rostnikov thought, it had been a much longer night for Sonya Granovsky and her daughter—if she were still alive—and for Emil Karpo, and even for Ilyusha Malenko.

The sun had not yet come up, but Rostnikov's watch told him it was five in the morning. He looked at Tkach and was surprised to see the stubble of a yellow beard that made the junior inspector look even younger.

"Let's shave," Rostnikov said, clearing his throat. "I have a razor in a drawer here someplace."

Rostnikov leaned over to open a drawer and discovered that the pain in his leg had neither gone away nor eased. He found the razor and handed it to Tkach, who took it with a nod and left the room.

As soon as he was gone, Rostnikov picked up the

phone and called his home. Sarah answered before the second ring.

"I'm still in the office," he said quietly. "I couldn't tell you last night, but I have reason to believe that Iosef may be on his way back to Kiev or possibly on his way here."

"How could you . . ." she began and stopped. "I don't care. Is it true?"

"I think so," he said quietly. "We'll know soon."

"What did you have to do to get this information?" Sarah said with sympathy.

"Nothing I don't have to do every day of my life," he said. "Now I must go back to work. I'll let you know if anything . . . if I learn more."

"You'll be careful, Porfiry," she said.

"About what?" he chuckled.

"I don't know," said his wife and hung up.

Tkach came back in five minutes, clean-shaven and bearing hot tea and hard rolls. Rostnikov ate quickly and took the razor.

"Can I use the phone to call my wife?" he asked Rostnikov, who limped painfully to the door.

"Call," said Rostnikov.

His leg would not bend without great pain, so he marched stiff-legged past the desks of the few junior officers who were either still on duty from the night before or had come in early. A phone rang, and Zelach picked it up about fifteen feet in front of the slow-moving Rostnikov.

"Yes," came the officer's voice. "I understand. The location. Yes. Inspector." Zelach had his hand over the mouthpiece as he called to Rostnikov. "I think we have a woman on the phone who had her car taken by Malenko.''

Rostnikov hobbled over to the desk and grabbed the phone.

"Yes," he said swiftly.

"My name is Vera Alleyanovskya, and my car was stolen last night by a mad young man with a young girl."

"Where did this happen and why didn't you call us earlier?" Rostnikov said, motioning for Zelach to go to his office and get Tkach.

"I almost died in the woods," she explained. "Some people on a farm took me in. They had no phone."

"Tell me where you are, and I'll have a man out there to pick you up immediately."

She told him, and Rostnikov hung up just as Tkach moved to his side.

"Another chance, Sasha," he said. "Take Zelach and a car and find this woman whose car was stolen. Try to follow Malenko's trail." Tkach nodded and motioned for Zelach to get his coat.

What, thought Rostnikov, is Malenko doing out there? The thinking of this madman still eluded him. He headed for the washroom, to shave. He would worry later about thinking.

By six in the morning, Emil Karpo was prepared for surgery. He lay in the preparation room next to another patient, a woman who, he heard, had a stomach cancer. They said nothing to each other. Karpo's arm had ceased to hurt. It had no feeling at all, which allowed Karpo to channel his thoughts elsewhere.

"Emil," came a voice through his thoughts. He

looked up at Rostnikov, whose eyes were heavy with sleeplessness.

"Inspector," said Karpo, his mouth surprisingly dry. He tried to lick his lips but there was no moisture. "They are going to take the arm."

"I know Emil," said Rostnikov.

"It will be a great inconvenience," said Karpo, growing drowsy.

Rostnikov laughed. The sick woman prepared for surgery looked at him, as did a male nurse.

"A great inconvenience," agreed Rostnikov. "I've asked Procurator Timofeyeva to assign us together permanently. You are too valuable an officer to lose over a disability. Many of us operate under disabilities. My leg . . ."

"I will be pleased to serve with you," said Karpo, fighting sleep. "But there is something else. Something I have figured out that will be of value. How long will I be asleep from this procedure?"

"The doctor tells me it will be six or more hours before you can speak," whispered Rostnikov.

"Too long," said Karpo, his voice fading. Rostnikov had to lean forward to hear his words. "The sickle."

"The sickle?"

"Yes," said Karpo weakly, "the sickle. A rusty sickle and a rusty hammer. We thought it was political, but the hammer and sickle are more than a symbol. They are a symbol of something. The union of agriculture and labor. And you said Malenko was carrying a rusty scissors. Hammer, sickle, scissors. Tools, old farm tools. They are not political symbols. They are memories of his childhood. He was raised on a farm until he was ten, his father's farm.''

"How can you remember such things?" Rostnikov shook his head.

"My job," said Karpo, his voice fading. "My job." And he was asleep.

Rostnikov moved away and took a doctor by the arm. The doctor was busy and glared at the inspector. But something in the heavy man's eyes and the firmness of his grip made the doctor stop and pay attention.

"Is his life in danger?" asked Rostnikov softly.

"Yes," said the doctor, who was dark and seemed foreign in some way. "But he will most likely survive. He is a very strong, determined man."

"Yes," agreed Rostnikov, letting the doctor's arm go.

Rostnikov left the hospital and got back into his waiting car. Michael Veselivitch Dolguruki turned on the engine and drove into the street.

"May I ask Chief Inspector, how Sergeant Karpo is?" said Dolguruki.

"Yes," said Rostnikov. "He is improving."

Ten minutes later Rostnikov was at the office of Sergei Malenko's factory. It was a large factory with machines and a modest office, but Malenko was not in the office. His secretary, a young man, informed Rostnikov reluctantly that Malenko was at a meeting with some foreigners at the Praga Restaurant. Rostnikov was welcome to wait, but Rostnikov had no intention of waiting. Natasha Granovsky might still be alive. He went out of the factory and stepped into the silence of the street. It was only then that he realized how noisy the factory had been and understood why Sergei Malenko had been so slow to respond to him during the interview at his *dacha*. He was probably partly deaf. The price Malenko had paid for his success was mounting.

Rostnikov felt uncomfortable at the Praga Resturant. He did not normally go to resturants. Only once a year did he, his wife and Iosef go to a restaurant and that only on Iosef's birthday. It had been delayed this year because Iosef had been unable to obtain leave at his birthday.

The waiter at the door greeted Rostnikov and asked him if he wanted a seat.

"No," said Rostnikov, afraid that his leg would lock if he sat. "I am looking for Sergei Malenko. Police business. Tell him Inspector Rostnikov must see him."

"Very good, Inspector," said the man and walked away. Rostnikov stood in the small lobby, watching the lunch eaters and listening to the pleasant hum of soft conversation in the darkened dining room. Maybe he could afford to take Sarah and Iosef here. The extra weights could wait. He could make do for another year.

The waiter, a particularly thin man, came back with rapid step and came very close to Rostnikov.

"Comrade Malenko asks that you wait here. He will be done in no more than ten or fifteen minutes."

"In ten or fifteen minutes, a fourteen-year-old girl can be dead," said Rostnikov walking past the waiter and heading across the restaurant dining room toward the door from which the waiter had come after bringing Malenko's message. He bumped into a chair protruding into the aisle, and a man with a dark suit and black eyes turned to say something and then changed his mind.

Rostnikov did not hesitate at the door behind which he heard voices. Nor did he knock. He pushed it open and found himself facing five men seated around a table. One of the men was Sergei Malenko, who stopped in mid-sentence and stood up angrily.

"You will have to wait, Inspector," he said.

The table was set with a bottle of Stolichnaya vodka, caviar, baked veal, and potatoes steaming in the well heated private room.

"I cannot wait," he said firmly. "I am sorry, gentlemen."

"These gentlemen cannot understand Russian," Malenko said with a smile and a nod at the men.

"Good," said Rostnikov. "I need some answers from you very quickly."

"You will be sorry for this, Rostnikov," Malenko said without losing his smile.

"Not as sorry as you will be if you fail to answer me."

"Ask your questions quickly and then leave," said Malenko patiently.

"You lived on a farm before all this," said Rostnikov.

"That was a long time ago," said Malenko. "Eighteen, twenty years ago."

"That was where your child was killed by your wife?"

"Yes," said Malenko, unable to keep up his false front and glaring at the policeman.

"Where is that farm?"

"North of the city, beyond Druzhba. A farmer

named Breask or something like that owns it. Why do you ask?''

"I think," said Rostnikov, "that your son may be heading there. I think he may have kept some tools of yours from that farm and is now using them to kill people, kill people who he thinks betrayed him. Does that make sense to you?''

"No," said Malenko, his dark face turning pale.

The four other men in the room looked at the two antagonists in confusion.

"He has a young girl with him," said Rostnikov. "Give me complete directions for getting to the farm, and give them to me quickly.''

Rostnikov handed a notebook and pencil to Malenko, who sketched a map and handed it back to the policeman.

"Thank you. Would you like to come?''

"No," said Malenko sitting back down. "I . . . no.''

Rostnikov turned and left the room.

Tkach and Zelach had found the abandoned car with the help of directions from Vera Alleyanovskya. Forty minutes later they found the trail of footprints in the snow. It was faint and had been obscured here and there by falling and drifting snow, but it could be followed.

"This is ridiculous," mumbled Zelach an hour later. Their car had been left on the road behind Vera Alleyanovskya's vehicle, and with each step they moved further and further from it.

"But necessary," replied Tkach, moving forward.

An hour later they found the farmhouse where

Malenko and the girl had stopped and they found the reluctant farmer.

"I'll talk," Tkach whispered to Zelach as they approached the man who stood in the door, axe in hand.

"Comrade," shouted Tkach, letting a sob enter his voice. "We are looking for my little sister. She was taken by force by a man she doesn't want to marry. We have reason to believe he brought her this way."

"Go to the police," the farmer said, fingering his axe.

"The police," cried Tkach. "I want nothing to do with the police. This is a private matter, a matter of honor."

"The police are trouble," agreed the farmer looking suspiciously at Zelach.

"My brother," Tkach explained.

The man nodded.

"The man looked a bad sort," the farmer said. "Girl did look frightened. He asked me how to get to a village near here. Come in. I'll tell you where he went."

"Michael Veselivitch Dolguruki," sighed Rostnikov, "you are an outstanding driver. I applaud your skill under difficult conditions, but we can do the girl no good if we do not arrive at our destination."

The police *Volga* had careened down the highways and back roads into the late afternoon. On one occasion the car had come very near overturning on a skid. On another occasion, a remarkably fat woman had to leap off the road in front of the car with a dexterity that made Rostnikov blink with wonder.

"I'm sorry, Inspector," Dolguruki said, keeping his

eyes on the road, "but I thought you told me to hurry."

"Hurry, hurry," sighed Rostnikov, waving his hand in the air.

Rostnikov was worried about the girl, true, but he was also worried about how he might explain the destruction of the automobile. His body and that of the driver could be repaired by doctors. Doctors in Moscow were good and there would be no cost. But to repair an automobile. Ah, thought, Rostnikov, that may be much more difficult.

With that thought, another car joined them on the narrow road and slid in front of them. Rostnikov's driver hit his brakes and went into a skid that appeared certain to result in crash into the second car. Rostnikov sucked in his breath, braced himself with his good leg, and gripped the door handle. The second car had stalled in front of them, and slow motion took over Rostnikov's consciousness. His car moved as if through water. The movement took the length of a war and the time of a sneeze, but ended without a collision.

Rostnikov and his driver leaped out to confront the other car's occupants. There was no more than an inch or two between the cars.

"Tkach!" Rostnikov shouted, watching his breath form a cloud.

"*Inspector!*" shouted Tkach back as he stepped out of his car. Behind the young detective, Rostnikov could see the outline of Zelach. "We know the village where Malenko has taken the girl."

"And you think I am just riding around out here to witness the magnificent efforts of farmers preparing their futures?" sighed the inspector.

"No, I—" began Tkach.

"Never mind," Rostnikov interrupted. "Let's turn your car and get it going in the right direction. "Zelach," he shouted, "get behind the wheel. We'll push."

Rostnikov, Tkach, and the driver pushed the car as Zelach gently started the engine. Its rear was firmly locked in a bank of snow blocking the road.

"Out of the way," Rostnikov shouted, pushing Tkach and Dolguruki. You, Zelach, out of the car."

"You have an idea, Inspector?"

"I have a challenge," Rostnikov grinned, but it was a grin without joy. Zelach scampered out of the car and joined them in the road. Far off the road was a house with a chimney puffing little clouds of grey smoke. Somewhere in the distance across the reaches of snow a cow bellowed, and on the road Rostnikov moved to the rear of the stalled car. He took off his gloves, rubbed his hands on his coat, concentrated, took three deep breaths, held the last and put his hands under the bumper. With knees bent and back straight, he began to lift, his face turning red with the effort, a dry chill freezing moisture on his nose. He imagined the extra weights he had been unable to purchase. He imagined himself at the park championships lifting for the first place medal, he imagined himself at the Olympic games breaking a world record, and he rose. He could feel the pressure in his groin and knew his bad leg was wobbling dangerously, but he rose. The rear of the car came up and he pushed forward, letting it go. The car bounced twice and rested free of the snow bank. Rostnikov gasped for air and tried to speak to cap his moment, but it was difficult to get the words out. Instead, he slumped forward and put one hand against the now free car and pulled in short gulps.

"Don't . . . stand . . . Let's get going." He waved his hand violently at the three men who watched him. Dolguruki, the driver, was the first to respond. He hurried to his car. Tkach and Zelach moved quickly into their car, and Rostnikov stood up to allow them to pull away. As they started up the road, Rostnikov shuffled back to his *Volga* and got in the front next to Dolguruki.

"You are deceptively strong, Inspector," said the driver starting the car. The car in front of them was clearly in sight.

"Is that a compliment?" asked Rostnikov, damning himself for being unable to catch his breath.

"Of course," said the driver.

Rostnikov shrugged.

Fifteen minutes later, both cars pulled into the village of Svenilaslav. The village itself was only slightly larger than a small farm and consisted of one two-story village store, a government grain trading center and a small brick one-story building that served as the village center.

Inside the brick building, Andrei Froskerov, who had recently celebrated his eighty-first birthday, was trying to decide if he was going to steal one of the chairs from the meeting room. He had stolen one a year earlier and sold it ten miles away to an engineer, but Comrade Scort had looked at him suspiciously for months. Not having been caught had given Andrei Forskerov courage. Besides, the engineer had told him that he could use a matching chair. He might even pay a few hundred kopecks. Froskerov was alone in the building, as he often was. His task was to keep it clean, which he did, and to protect village property, which he did not do.

He had definitely decided to take the chair and had one hand on it when the three men burst into the room. One was a burly man with a limp and the other two were young, determined-looking men.

"I wasn't taking it," cried Froskerov, recognizing policemen when he saw them. "I was cleaning it."

"Cleaning it?" asked Tkach.

"Yes," said Froskerov, whipping a ragged cloth from his pocket and attacking the upholstered chair.

"That's nice," Rostnikov said softly. "You may continue to do that, old father, but we must know—"

"I've never taken anything from the village, from my country!" cried Froskerov as he vigorously worked at the material with his cloth. "I'd rather die, here on the spot: May God strike me down. Wait, there is no God anymore. Forgive me, I'm an old man, but I'm a good worker."

Tkach looked at Zelach who looked at Rostnikov who spoke softly.

"Malenko."

"Malenko," agreed the old man.

"You remember Malenko?" Rostnikov went on. "You were in this village when he was a farmer."

"Ha," shouted the quivering old man. "I have always lived here. I've been here all my life except for the war. The Germans got me. I was a prisoner in some place in Poland. I have a scar."

With this he threw his cloth on the table and lifted his

shirt to reveal a ridged scar that went from his navel to his scrawny rib cage.

"You are a hero of the state," said Rostnikov. "Malenko."

"I knew him," said the old man, tucking his shirt in.

"Where was his farm? Where is it? Who lives on it?"

"It is not his farm," said Froskerov. "It went to the collective and then Max Rodnini. I didn't think he should get it," the old man whispered loudly. "He's really a Hungarian, but no one asked me then and no one asks me now, and I am not one to give my advice to those who do not want it. Eighty years of experience should count for something."

"He could be killing the girl right now," Tkach whispered frantically.

Rostnikov put up a hand to quiet the detective.

"Killing? Who?" Froskerov said looking into the three faces in panic. "Rodnini, the Hungarian? I knew he'd kill that wife of his some day. I saw her hit him once with—"

"Father," Rostnikov tried again. "You must tell us now, right now, how to get to Rodnini's farm. You must tell us and we will go, or I must ask you what you were taking from here when we came in."

"Taking, taking?" laughed the old man. "Me taking? Ha. Don't make me laugh."

"Rodnini. *Now*," demanded Rostnikov.

"Down the road, to the right, second farm, the one with the broken truck in the driveway."

"Thank you, old father," Rostnikov said, turning.

Froskerov looked puzzled.

"Are they rounding up Hungarians?" he asked, but he got no answer. The three policemen were out of the door. He thought he should inform someone about this curious visit but could think of no one to tell. The members of the village council were on their farms except for storekeeper Putsko, who was in Moscow picking up supplies. He would tell Putsko when he returned, if he could remember all of what had happened. He sat heavily in the chair that he had planned to steal and began working out the story of how Rodnini had murdered his wife and been carted away by three policemen who were rounding up Hungarians for a purge. Under the circumstances, he certainly could not steal the chair, at least not for another few days.

The sun was behind the cloud cover on its way down when the two cars stopped. They were several hundred yards from the farm and could clearly see the wreck of a truck in the driveway. The truck was a model Rostnikov had been taught to drive when he had been in the army, but he had never had the opportunity to get behind the wheel.

The meeting in the road was chilled by a rising wind across the fields that sent swirls of loose snow dancing on the packed, unbroken surface.

The two junior inspectors and the driver looked at Rostnikov, who was tempted to ask what they thought should be done. He could see by their faces, however, that they expected their superior, who could lift automobiles, to come up with a plan. Rostnikov had none.

"He is certainly here by now if he is coming," he said, stalling.

Tkach nodded in agreement.

"If we go driving up to the farm, he could see us and kill the girl and the Rodninis," he went on.

"So," sighed Roṣtnikov. "We can't simply sit here either. I will walk to the house. Malenko has never seen me. Perhaps he will take me for a neighbor. We can't get too close or he will recognize the police cars. I'll walk from here. Make a bundle out of things in the trunk, a light bundle but a big one. Maybe he will take me for a neighbor or a peddler."

Dolguruki hurried to open the trunk of the car and prepare a bundle.

"If either of you has another idea . . ." he began, thinking that his own plan was, at best adequate, at worst stupid. Neither detective had an idea.

"I think I should go with you," ventured Tkach.

Rostnikov looked at him evenly.

"He has seen you," Rostnikov reminded him.

"I'd cover my face."

Doguruki returned with a heavy blanket tied with rope and folded over. Rostnikov took it and hoisted it to his shoulder.

"Give me half an hour, no more. If you do not see me or hear from me by then, I want the three of you to make your way across the field behind the house and use your judgment. You understand, Sasha?"

"I understand, Inspector."

"Good," said Rostnikov. "Now, we shall see."

With that he started down the road. The bundle was light, and Rostnikov welcomed its rough warmth against his face. He tried to think of a plan, but no plan came to mind. He would simply do what had to be done. There was not even any point in hoping for the safety of the girl. She was either alive or dead. Rostnikov's interest turned to Ilyusha Malenko. He had come to know the young man superficially in the last two days and wanted a direct contact—a look at the eyes, the body, the movement, a sense of the smell and feel of the man—to understand his madness. The walk was deliberately slow. He did not want to appear in a hurry. Slow, slow. A neighbor returning a tool. He tried to whistle but his mouth was dry, and the vision of Karpo raced across his consciousness.

The farm was small, a two-story wooden house with a barn about thirty yards behind it. The path to the house was not shoveled, but someone had come up it. Rostnikov could not make out if the footprints were of two people.

By the time he got to the front door, his heart was beating furiously, and his leg needed a long massage. He tried to force the whistle out, but nothing came, so he knocked.

"Comrade Rodnini," he shouted in what he hoped was a friendly neighbor's tone. "It is I, Porfiry."

There was no answer. Rostnikov set down his bundle and knocked again, but still there was no answer. Then he tried the door and it was unlocked. He went in.

"Rodnini?" he said with a smile on his face.

There were no lights in the house. The room into which he stepped was a large combination dining room, kitchen, and living room. A large rough-hewn grey rug was on the floor. An old sofa stood in one corner and a heavy table beside it. On the walls were farm tools.

Malenko had clearly been here. Furniture was broken. A window above the dining table was out, and the wind sprinkled the room with drifting snow and sent the sun-bleached curtains billowing into the room.

There was no blood, but neither was there any sign of life.

"Rodnini?" he shouted, and above him Rostnikov heard a sound of someone or something. He moved to the narrow stairs and looked up into the darkness.

"It is I, Porfiry," he said. "Did you and *mamalushka* have another quarrel?" He laughed as he moved up the stairs, slowly trying to pick form out of shadow. At the top of the stairs, he braced himself for an attack. None came and he looked around. There were only two rooms, neither of which had doors. The sound came from the larger of the two rooms, a bedroom. Rostnikov stepped in and looked around without moving, as his eyes adjusted. The sound came from behind a door across the small room. Rostnikov moved to it, took the handle and pulled, his free hand and arm ready to ward off an attack, but again no attack came. On the floor lay two human figures. Rostnikov kneeled and pulled them out into the bedroom. Both were bound and gagged, and the man was looking around wildly with amazingly blue eyes. The woman's eyes were closed and a dark gash bubbled blood from her scalp. Both were in their sixties, heavy and small. Rostnikov pulled the gag from the man's mouth.

"Where is he?" Rostnikov asked softly.

The man coughed and gagged.

"He broke in . . . began breaking things. My wife tried to stop him. It was so fast. He hit her in the head and me in the stomach. He is mad, crazy."

"I know," Rostnikov soothed. "But where is he now?"

"I don't know. I don't know," cried the man. Then he looked at the still form of his wife. "Is she dead?"

"I don't think so," said Rostnikov, moving to the woman.

"Oh," wailed the man, but Rostnikov couldn't tell if he was relieved or disappointed.

"Go out on the road," Rostnikov ordered, "toward town. There are two cars and some men. We are the police. Tell them to come and get your wife. You understand?"

"Yes," said the man, standing on weak legs. He looked back at his wife and stood transfixed.

"Go," ordered Rostnikov and the man fled down the stairs. Rostnikov checked the woman's eyes and listened to her breathing. He couldn't tell if the labored sound was from asthma or trauma. He put her on the bed and went to the window to see if he could see Tkach from the farm. He could and he could see the farmer Rodnini hurrying through the snow to the road, slipping and falling in his haste. Rostnikov could also see two clear sets of footprints leading from the house to the barn. He squinted out the window with his head cocked to see if he could see footsteps leading away from the barn, but there were none.

Rostnikov went down the stairs and out the front door into the snow. There could be no more surprise, no tricks, and so there was no great reason to move slowly, but then again his body and leg did not encourage rapid movement. Yes, the footprints were clear and fresh and not in his mind. He looked at the small barn but could see no face at the window. He moved to the door and opened it slowly.

"Ilyusha," he said firmly.

Something stirred inside, and he heard a clear whimper. The barn was chilly but there was no wind breaking through.

"Ilyusha Malenko, I know you are here," he repeated, stepping in and seeing nothing but a cow in the corner, some small sheds, and a dozen chickens looking at him with curiosity.

"Father?" came a young man's voice from one of the sheds.

"No," replied Rostnikov, moving forward slowly.

"Who is it?" demanded the voice.

"My name is Rostnikov," he said. "Porfiry Rostnikov. I am a policeman."

The shed was low, and Rostnikov stepped to where he could see over the rough wooden slat at the top.

"Stop," shouted Malenko, and Rostnikov stopped. Huddled in the corner of the shed on a bed of grain were two people, a whimpering young man with wild blond hair and frightened eyes who held a knife to a girl's throat. The man wore heavy black pants and a workman's shirt. The girl wore absolutely nothing.

"I've stopped," said Rostnikov. "I have a message from your father."

"He is good at having other people deliver his messages," Malenko laughed.

"If you don't want it . . ." Rostnikov shrugged.

"What is it?" The knife touched the girl's throat and she coughed.

"The girl is very sick," Rostnikov said. "Can we put my coat on her?"

"My father's message," demanded Malenko, his eyes darting wildly to the window in search of more police.

"He wants you to know that he will support you in your trial. That he is sorry for a great deal and finds it ironic that it should take events such as these to bring you together," Rostnikov lied.

"Too late," said Malenko, shifting his weight slightly.

"Why is it too late?" Rostnikov said taking another step forward. "Maybe the worst you'll get with his help is ten years of *buterskalia ichurmo,* hard labor."

"Stop. Stop. Stop. Stop," screamed Malenko scrambling to his knees, his knife constantly at the pulsing throat of the girl. His movement caused a slight, thin cut and the girl's face distorted in fear. Rostnikov looked away and then back quickly.

"I've stopped. Let us talk."

"No time for talk," said Malenko. "There'll be more of you soon and you'll shoot me down. I know the police."

"We'll not shoot you down," Rostnikov said evenly. "And there is time for nothing but talk. You killed—"

"Marie and Granovsky—her father," Malenko said looking at the girl's frightened face.

"And the cab driver," Rostnikov added.

"He didn't count," said Malenko.

Rostnikov shrugged.

"We can debate that another time," he went on. "But what do you want with the girl? Why do you want to harm her?"

"You don't understand," Malenko cried in despair

at the policeman's ignorance. "I'm not going to kill her. I'm going to do with her what her father did with my wife. Then . . ."

"What was that?" Rostnikov asked, thinking only of keeping the drama at the level of conversation as he tried to inch his way forward.

"You know. You know. She knows. He was supposed to be my friend. She . . . You know what they did behind my back. He was in my bed. They laughed at me. Now they are dead, and I will laugh at them." He did, indeed, laugh.

"That is not the happiest laugh I have heard," commented Rostnikov.

"That's because there is no joy in it," the young man sobbed.

"It is a laugh we Russians have known for a thousand years," said Rostnikov.

"And the girl?"

"Her father is going to kill her after I finish. No, I am not mad, or perhaps I am. He will kill her by the chain of events he started when he and Marie . . ."

"But he will never know," interrupted Rostnikov. "He is dead, unless you believe in some religion of spirits or souls."

"I don't care if he knows, don't you see," explained Malenko, taking the knife briefly from the girl's throat to point it at himself. "I know. That is enough. That is all that counts."

"I see," nodded Rostnikov. "I shall watch with curiosity. You plan to rape this sick girl and then kill her, all with one hand. For surely, if you put down the knife, you will have to contend with me."

"I'll manage," he said. "I'll manage, and if I can't, I'll simply kill her."

"You didn't manage so well with her mother," Rostnikov whispered. "Is that a general problem you have, Ilyusha?"

"You want me to kill her? Is that what you want? Is that why you taunt me? Are you crazy, policeman? Will it simply be easier to kill me once I kill her? Do you just want to get this over so you can get back to your dinner?"

"Many questions, Ilyusha," he said. "I don't want you to kill her. I want to take her to a hospital. Look at what you have done to her, and she was not in conspiracy with her father to harm you. I know you are mad, but even within your madness you should be able to recognize logic when you hear it."

"I used to live here," Malenko shouted, putting the knife to the young girl's stomach. His eyes moved around the barn. "I used to sleep in this barn with my brother when I was young, and we used to talk and watch the room grow . . . and I told him stories."

"You brother died when he was an infant. Your mother killed him," Rostnikov said.

"You are a fool, policeman," screamed Malenko. "Don't they train you to humor people like me, not to provoke them?"

"Ilyusha, may I lean on the railing? I have a very bad leg from the war and I cannot stand like this for long."

Malenko looked confused and Rostnikov ambled slowly another step and leaned on the rail four or five feet from the two figures. The girl was shivering with fever and fear.

"Thank you," sighed Rostnikov. "You were saying?"

"Don't provoke me."

"I won't." Rostnikov held up his right hand. "I don't want to provoke you. I am just a weary cripple who would like to understand a situation which has gotten far away from him. Can I ask you a question?"

"A question?" Malenko tried to pull himself and the girl further into the corner of the shed. The grain shifted under them, and the sound made the chickens behind Rostnikov scurry with excitement.

"How did you find out about your wife and Granovsky? Did you catch them?"

Malenko's head nodded, and his body shook with emotion. Rostnikov realized that he was on the verge of action or breaking.

"He told me."

"Granovsky told you?"

"No, a man, a friend, a member . . . a friend."

Rostnikov shook his head in disbelief.

"No, no one told you. You're starting to tell lies again. You had no evidence for what you did."

"He told me," Malenko insisted pointing the knife at the policeman. "Fero Dolonick told me. He saw them. He had a photograph. He showed me."

Rostnikov scratched his head and tried not to look at the frightened face of the girl.

"He had photographs of your wife and Granovsky? Did you ask him how he got them?"

"I didn't care. He had them. It was true. Aleksander came to see her the day I killed him. I waited. I saw him go in. I saw. No more talk. No more pain."

Malenko's eyes were filled with moisture, and his free hand went up to cover his ears.

"May I make a practical suggestion?" Rostnikov said, leaning forward.

Malenko wiped his sleeve across his eyes. The cow mooed behind them.

"I suggest," said Rostnikov, "that before you attempt to get your clothes off and rape the girl that you put me out of the way. It will make your task much easier."

"This is a trick," smiled Malenko, his eyes going to the window and door.

"Of course," agreed Rostnikov, "but not a very promising one on my part. I am tired, unable to move, unarmed, slow. You are young and, I understand, a madman has enormous strength. You seem quite mad to me. Consider it, Ilyusha. Or better yet, consider simply giving up. You have done enough. You have won your victory."

Malenko seemed to be considering the choices. He pursed his lips and got to his knees.

"And you young Natasha, what do you think?" Malenko said to the girl who had followed none of the conversation. "Perhaps I won't kill you. Perhaps, to have you will be enough. I'll—"

He turned and leaped at Rostnikov with the knife before him. Rostnikov had been ready, but had not anticipated the speed of movement from Malenko. The knife blade scraped along the top of his skull, opening a long thin cut and sending Rostnikov sprawling backward onto an unwitting chicken which was crushed beneath his body. Malenko came over the top of the shed, and Rostnikov brought up his good leg to kick at the young man. The kick caught Malenko's shoulder and sent him sprawling across the barn into the legs of the frightened cow. Chickens went wild, and Rostnikov tried to rise. His own blood blinded him, and Malenko was on him again.

Rostnikov caught the hand with the knife and pushed it back. The young man grunted and struggled and threw his knee toward Rostnikov's groin, but the policeman turned sideways, taking the knee against his thigh. Rostnikov grabbed for the young man's leg and caught it at the thigh. With one hand gripping the arm with the knife and the other squeezing into the young man's shoulder, Rostnikov lifted. Malenko weighed at least one hundred fifty-five pounds, a simple bench press with a dead weight, a bit difficult with living, unevenly distributed weight. With a tensing of his shoulders Rostnikov prepared to throw Malenko into the shed door and end the battle.

Then something exploded in the room. For an instant Rostnikov thought that the wound to his head had been more severe than he had sensed, that he must be suffering some kind of hemhorrage, but the sound cleared and Malenko's body went limp. Still holding the limp form over his head, Rostnikov tried to see through his own blood and had only the image of Malenko wearing a red mask. He dropped the body and rolled over.

"Are you all right?" came a voice. Rostnikov wiped his face with his sleeve and turned toward the barn door, where he could see a man in a policeman's uniform. It was Dolguruki, the driver. A gun was in his hand.

"I am all right," said Rostnikov, struggling to his knees. "You did not have to kill im."

"He had a knife," said Dolguruki, stepping toward the body. A crowd of chickens followed him.

"Yes," said Rostnikov, pulling himself up and removing his coat.

He looked over the top of the shed at the girl, who cowered back when she saw his bloody face.

"It's nothing," he said. "A scratch. You are all right now. We'll get you to a hospital." He handed her his coat and she grabbed for it and hugged it to her thin body.

"He's dead," said Dolguruki, kneeling at the body.

"I'm not surprised," said Rostnikov, opening the shed to help the girl.

Tkach and Zelach ran into the barn, guns drawn, to take in the sight. Zelach's eyes went from the body of Malenko to that of the crushed chicken. Tkach looked with horror at Rostnikov.

"It's a deep scratch," Rostnikov explained, looking around for something to stop the bleeding as he lifted the girl in his arms. He could feel the warmth of her fever right through his coat.

"Does it hurt?" said Tkach.

"Only when I think," replied Rostnikov, looking at Doguruki and the sprawled body of Ilyusha Malenko. "Only when I think. Now we must get her to a hospital."

CHAPTER THIRTEEN

Emil Karpo had a dream. In the dream, he was floating on his back, absolutely stiff, as if he had been hypnotized by a magician. He was quite comfortable and mildly surprised to see the magician hovering over him. He was even more surprised that the white turbaned magician looked exactly like Porfiry Rostnikov. Rostnikov looked as if he were deep in concentration to insure the success of his trick, and Karpo wanted to insure that the trick would indeed work.

"What can I do?" Karpo mumbled in his dream.

Rostnikov touched his arm, and Karpo started. It was not a dream. Rostnikov did hover over him in a turban. He also discovered that it was true that one had the illusion that one could feel an amputated limb. Karpo, had not logic stayed him, could have sworn that he felt Rostnikov touch his non-existent arm.

"Turban?" Karpo mumbled dryly through the first sign of coming out of the anesthetic.

Rostnikov touched the bandage and shook his head, no.

"Wounded, stitches, twenty-seven," he said. "We got Malenko. And there is a tale to tell. How are you feeling?"

Karpo looked around the room. A man in the bed next to him looked away.

"My arm," he said.

"Is still there," said Rostnikov. "A surgeon with a cancelled operation decided to spend four hours on you, putting little pieces back together, rebuilding your bones with little leftover pieces. He is quite proud of what he has done. You will have a little difficulty with it, but you should be using it again in a matter of months. The doctor predicted six months. I told him it would be two."

"It will be one," corrected Karpo in a whisper, feeling himself sink back into sleep.

When he woke up again, there was no one in the room. He tried to move his injured arm but could not. He could, however, feel some tingling in his fingers. Minutes or an hour later, the man in the next bed returned. He said nothing to Karpo, and Karpo said nothing to him. The man, a bricklayer, tried not to look at the tall man beside him who never blinked, but it was an effort. After a while, the vision of Karpo proved too much for him, and the man made an excursion out of the room, almost bumping into Rostnikov and Tkach on the way.

"You are awake," observed Rostnikov. Karpo looked at him. Tkach nodded, and Karpo nodded back. The two visitors moved close to the bed. Something was clearly on their minds.

"We have a problem, Emil, a problem indeed that the three of us must be aware of," whispered Rostnikov.

Karpo's brow furrowed, and he turned his full attention to the inspector, whose turban had been replaced by a piece of white tape through a patch of shaved scalp.

"I'll give you the facts," said Rostnikov sitting on the side of the bed. "You draw the conclusions. Before he died, Ilyusha Malenko said that he had been told by a friend named Dolonick that his wife and Granovsky were lovers. Dolonick had shown him a photograph of them, given him evidence. I attempted to find this Dolonick. He is a writer who has been friendly with several leading dissidents including Granovsky. He is now unfindable. I called the K.G.B. and left a message for Colonel Drozhkin to call me. Ten minutes later a call came that the colonel was not available. Five minutes after that, Procurator Timofeyeva called to order me to her office this evening and told me to talk to no one about this incident."

Karpo's eyes remained fixed on Rostnikov's face. Rostnikov reached up to touch his bandage to be sure it had not departed.

"There is more," said Rostnikov looking up at Tkach, who stood pale and listened. "Malenko was shot by a police officer named Dolguruki who was serving as my driver. He took over from another driver who was supposedly ill. I checked on the earlier driver. He was not ill. He had simply been transfered to other duties. I attempted to find Dolguruki but was told that he had been sent to Tbilisi on a special assignment. I did not question that it was unusual to send uniformed officers from Moscow on special assignment to Tbilisi. The conclusion?''

"Yes," said Karpo. "But I'm sure there was a reason, a good reason."

"Oh, yes," agreed Rostnikov, "a very good reason. The K.G.B. asks an agent posing as a dissident to find a way to get rid of Granovsky before his trial, before he can cause international embarrassment. The agent, Dolonick, knows about Granovsky's affair with Marie Malenko. He also knows of Malenko's instability and begins playing on it, prodding Malenko to act. To set the stage, Granovsky is allowed to be free and guarded only by one incompetent K.G.B. agent. Malenko kills Granovsky and we are called in to find Malenko and prove that the killing is totally nonpolitical. When Vonovich came up, the K.G.B. was quite satisfied to go with him and let Malenko go, but Malenko was out of control and had killed two more. And we refused to stop the pursuit of Malenko and kept tying it in to the Granovsky murder. And so the K.G.B. arranged for a man who would serve as my driver and be ready to get rid of Malenko as soon as he was found to avoid any talking about Dolonick, who had prodded Ilyusha Malenko to the killing.''

"Perhaps it had to be that way," said Karpo softly but firmly. "Granovsky's import goes beyond such simple questions as right and wrong."

"You believe that?" Tkach said.

"Yes," said Karpo, but Rostnikov noticed the pause before the sick man's answer, which Tkach did not catch and which Karpo would have covered had he been well.

"In any case," Rostnikov said, rising from the bed, "I thought you should know primarily because I must insure that no further inquiries are made. The case is closed. The murderer has been caught. Malenko killed his wife and kidnapped Natasha Granovsky. Vonovich, the drunken anti-revolutionary lout, killed Granovsky and the cab driver."

"And the girl?"

"She is recovering," sighed Rostnikov, touching his head again. "Her body is recovering well."

Rostnikov moved to the door with Tkach at his side.

"Goodnight, Inspector Karpo," said Rostnikov.

"I will be at work in one month," said Karpo.

"I know," said Rostnikov going out the door.

Rostnikov and Tkach stopped at a Stolovaya for a bowl of soup. They said little and took the metro back to Petrovka.

"And?" said Tkach when they returned to Rostnikov's office, where the inspector gathered his notes for his meeting with Procurator Anna Timofeyeva.

"And we go on working," said Rostnikov. "Do you see a resemblance between the scar on my desk and the one on my head? Curious."

"Yes," agreed Tkach. "Curious."

"Perhaps you and your wife would like to have dinner with my wife and me tomorrow night," said Rostnikov, looking intently at the autopsy report on the cab driver and wondering if he should bring it with him to his meeting with Anna Timofeyeva.

"Tomorrow, I . . . yes, I'm sure that would be fine."

"Nothing elaborate," warned Rostnikov.

"Thank you, comrade, we will be looking forward to it," Tkach said with a small smile.

"You did well, Sasha," said Rostnikov.

Before Tkach could consider an answer Rostnikov was gone. He could hear the older man's limping footsteps on the outer office floor. Tkach rubbed his stubbly face. He would stop at a liquor store on the way for a bottle of wine. It would surely delay him, especially if there was a long line, but Tkach wanted to celebrate, or perhaps he wanted to hide from what had happened in the last days. He wasn't at all sure which was which.

I must be tired, he thought to himself, but he did not really think it was so.

Anna Timofeyeva sat behind her desk, hands folded. This time she was not working on the stack of papers on her desk. This time her full attention was fixed on Porfiry Rostnikov, who hobbled in and nodded.

"You look terrible, Porfiry," she said.

She looked even worse to Rostnikov. Her face was pale and she looked more tired than he thought it was possible for a human being to look. He considered inviting her over for dinner too, but knew she would reject it and might even think it was an attempt to gain influence. It was not done to invite superiors to dinner. It was too suspicious.

Rostnikov waited till she motioned him to sit down. He did and put his file on her desk.

"I have all the papers." He began taking the reports out to hand to her but she stopped him.

"That was a foolish thing to do, Porfiry," she said.

He leaned back and rubbed his face with his right hand. The call to the K.G.B. was obviously at issue.

"There are times," she said carefully, "when it is best to forget about being a policeman and accept political truth and expediency."

"Yes, comrade," he said.

"You are a good policeman, Porfiry Rostnikov," she said slowly. "Will this report indicate that you are also one who can accept political compromise?"

"I present you with the evidence, Comrade Procurator. That is my function. It is up to you to draw conclusions." The chill of the room went through his back.

"That is true," she said, reaching her short arm across the table for the report file. Her uniform buttons were shiny and caught the light. "I think it best that you not testify at the trial of the cab driver, Vonovich. I don't think it will be necessary."

"Nor do I, comrade," he said.

"Granovsky's wife insists that her husband's murder was political, was somehow an act of the state," said

Anna Timofeyeva, looking through the file, "but the evidence of the case is quite clear and will be so even to foreign journalists. You have done well, Porfiry, and you deserve a rest."

"I would like one, comrade, a brief one," he said.

"And I would like to grant you one, but I'm afraid I need your services. An American staying at the Metropole Hotel has been murdered. It looks like a routine case, but . . ."

"It is politically awkward," said Rostnikov.

"Let's hope not," smiled Procurator Timofeyeva. "Let us hope not."

"And I assume I can use Tkach and Karpo if he is back on duty before we have the murderer?"

"Yes," said Timofeyeva handing him the police report on the dead American and turning back to her pile of work.

Rostnikov tucked the file under his arm and made his way back to his office. Malenko, the K.G.B., the corpse of Granovsky and that of Marie Malenko drifted into the file of unconsciousness, ready to come out when least expected. Tangible and dancing in his hand was the report on the murder of an American. An American.

Rostnikov's phone was ringing when he got to his office. It had been ringing as he walked through the outer office past the night shift of officers, but he did not hurry. When he got to it, he spoke evenly, efficiently, and with authority.

"Inspector Rostnikov," he said.

"Porfiry," came his wife's voice. "Iosef is back in Kiev. He just called."

The bloody face of Ilyusha Malenko leaped out of the darkness of memory and Rostnikov held back a surge of weakness.

"Good," he said, and his voice broke as he repeated, "good."

ABOUT THE AUTHOR

Stuart Kaminsky is the author of five Porfiry Rostnikov mysteries: DEATH OF A DISSIDENT, BLACK KNIGHT IN RED SQUARE (an Edgar nominee), RED CHAMELEON, A FINE RED RAIN, and the upcoming A COLD RED SUNRISE. He teaches film history, criticism, and production at Northwestern University, where he is a professor and head of the Division of Film. He lives in Skokie, Illinois, with his wife and three children.